# My Twisted Love Story

# My Twisted Love Story

ARUN SINGH

Srishti
PUBLISHERS & DISTRIBUTORS

**Srishti Publishers & Distributors**
A unit of AJR Publishing LLP
212A, Peacock Lane
Shahpur Jat, New Delhi – 110 049
editorial@srishtipublishers.com

First published by
Srishti Publishers & Distributors in 2022



10 9 8 7 6 5 4 3 2 1

This is a work of fiction. The characters, places, organisations and events described in this book are either a work of the author's imagination or have been used fictitiously. Any resemblance to people, living or dead, places, events, communities or organisations is purely coincidental.

The author asserts the moral right to be identified as the author of this work.

*I dedicate this book to*
*Divya, my wife;*
*Angel, my elder daughter*
*and Alishka, my little one.*

*"Take your broken heart, make it into art..."*

– Carrie Fisher to Meryl Streep

# Acknowledgement

I would like to extend my sincere gratitude to all those who inspired me to write this book.

My heartfelt gratitude for the blessings of Swami Ramdev Ji Maharaj for all my four books. His kind blessings and abundant love for my purpose of transforming the lives of people gives me indomitable courage to keep moving.

My gratitude to Dr Nagendra Neeraj, Chief Medical In-charge of Yog Gram for his constant inspiration and support to let my inspiring thoughts reach out to numerous people. Whenever we met, we used to go for long forest and nature trails. During these walks, we used to talk about life, health, mental wellness, laws of the universe and the way people should live their life to feel happy.

I am indebted to Dr Manju Neeraj, Pragya, Soumya and Medha for words of inspiration for all my writings. They have been my sounding board for all my books. I am grateful for their continued wishes and inspiration.

Thanks to Bishwamitra Singh, Urmila Singh, Sushil, Rajeev and Neelima for their motivating words, which went a long way in creating my second book.

Special credits to A.M. Misra, Former Chairman Tata Sponge, TSKZN, India Steel & Wire Products and Former Vice President HR Tata Steel, who has been a lifelong mentor and guide for me. As I said in my first book, I learnt from him that true and inspiring leaders exist in real life as well.

I would also like to mention a number of other people who played an instrumental role in my literary journey.

Mr U. Ramachandran, ex General Manager of Tata Steel Limited, who kept sending his kind words for me to write and publish books. Even after he moved to his native place in Kerala, he has always been in touch with me. His blessings and inspiration played a key role in making me an author. Often others' belief in our abilities is stronger than our self-belief. Mr Ramachandran has believed in me as an author for more than a decade now. Thank you sir!

Mr J.P. Bapat, Ex-Chief in Tata Steel Limited, who always admired my posts on Facebook. His words of encouragement finally made me write epics (I say this with humility) of human transformation in a gripping story format.

My friends from XLRI, Jamshedpur, Science College, Patna, and Birla Institute of Technology, Mesra, Ranchi, who have kept inspiring me.

Siji Raveendran, Transformation Mind Coach and Clinical Hypnotherapist for her valuable words of advice to make this book more powerful for transforming the life of readers.

Babuji, Ma and Jitendra bhaiya! Stay in peace wherever you are. I will fight with all my might to spread joys and success in the world around. Your goodness and blessings have made this possible.

My lovely wife Divya, for taking charge of the home front in the days of working from home. That gave me some time to complete the books by utilising my time, which I otherwise used to spend while driving to and back from office. Thank you for the months of hard work which you also put in along with me, in our respective areas.

Thanks to the entire team from Srishti Publishers, with a special mention of Arup, Stuti and Vini, for their constant and enduring support. They edited and polished the book to turn it into a gripping thriller of love and life.

And lastly, to everyone else who contributed to this book, whose name I might have missed mentioning. You are as important as the foundational pillars of a building. They are not always visible, but the building cannot stand without them.

Together, let's make this world happier, healthier and better.

With love,
Arun Singh

# A note from the author

This is my fifth book in less than one year. As I write these words, I am planning to write two more books which I call the 'motivational thrillers' of India.

Truly, we all have super powers; it is just that we often do not discover this power for long. I know for sure that many people don't get to discover this hidden power in life. I am grateful to the Universe for helping me to realise my powers, which were dormant within me. I had a seed of writing ingrained within me, which has now begun to turn into a tree.

*My Pietermaritzburg Moment* became a handbook of self-transformation to attain massive goals in life with the help of a mentor. The book elaborated on how 'adversity could become the mother of transformation'.

*The Strawberry Farm* is essentially a guide to reach greater success after experiencing setbacks in life, even without any mentor around. Both are in the form of a thrilling story and are known to give exhilarating moments to readers as they also reflect on their life while reading.

*Aroma of an Old Bakery* and *The Cliff Climber* left the readers with one key message – the world around us is full of magical lessons and secrets of success. Success leaves clues and these clues are everywhere around you. All you have to do is develop the mindset of a learner to understand these clues.

These stories are meant to awaken our conscience to such an extent that we learn the magic of staying inspired. This book is meant to keep you on the go, despite facing some of the most challenging moments in life.

*My Twisted Love Story* is my most ambitious project till date. 'Adversity is the mother of transformation' was the tagline of the book *My Pietermaritzburg Moment*. I replaced 'adversity' with the word 'breakup' as a breakup is nothing less than an adverse moment in someone's life.

Can someone use a breakup to transform one's life forever? The journey of finding the answer to this question led me to my fifth book, which is in your hands now.

Dive in and enjoy this exciting story!

# 1

# The Aroma of Coffee Beans

I am excited and nervous at the same time as I sit in Starbucks, waiting for her.

Analia Christopher is a journalist and biographer of national repute. She had been calling me over the last few days for a meeting in the café.

*But, why would a successful journalist want to talk to me? I am certainly not a big celebrity, even though I am in the making, so her sudden call was puzzling for me.*

From death to life, my journey has been a roller-coaster ride over the last few years. I have risen from the ashes to make my dreams come true. Just like a phoenix!

And, today is a big moment for me. After all, the famous Analia Christopher wants to interview *me*. I look at my watch. In my excitement to meet Analia, I arrived half an hour earlier. So, to pass time, I start looking around and keenly observe people and things. The rich and sweet aroma of coffee is tempting. All the tables along the walls overlooking the street are occupied. The glass walls give a clear view of the street surrounded by gulmohar trees.

It is late spring and flowers are in full bloom. Some of these flowers have fallen on the road and covered a part of it on both sides, as if they have a hidden message for pedestrians and drivers – that every living thing comes to an end someday.

On the road laden with flowers, I see people driving all types of vehicles, from ultra plush imported cars to leisurely Indian scooters. I also see many luxury cars on the street. Kasturgaon Park is a place of rich and the mighty. Pune is known as the automobile and manufacturing hub of India. Most of the visionaries, who created these organisations giving employment to thousands of people, live in these bungalows in Kasturgaon Park. The area also has a meditation centre run by an international group. You see many foreigners walking around in orange robes. I have never been able to get any hint of what goes inside the meditation centre. It is guarded against the prying eyes of onlookers.

I often used to go for a walk to the area and saw these bungalows. There is also a meditation garden beside a little *nallah* where one can go in the morning and evening hours. The garden is a good example of how a dirty place could be transformed into a beautiful landscape with flowers. Today, I know for sure that not only things, even people can be transformed completely. Again, it needs the vision of a coach who sees the potential of transformation in the mentee. Just like someone saw the potential in the place and transformed it by using the water of the same nallah which others might consider filthy. Life is all about the way we look at something. The day I learnt this lesson, my life changed forever.

As I ponder on these thoughts, I realize that it is just a few minutes till Analia arrives. She will be here anytime. I have exchanged a few emails with her in all these years, but I am going to meet her in person for the very first time today.

"Hey, Rohan! Sorry. Looks like you have been waiting for a while." Analia's animated voice came from behind. She has a powerful aura and charm, which is very impressive.

I greet her with a genuinely warm smile. We shake hands as she gracefully takes her seat on one of the tree trunk sofas kept along the way.

"So Rohan, first of all, let me give you a gift," she says.

"Gift? But I thought spending some time with you in this café is in itself a gift for me. I am wondering if there can be any better gift for me on this amazing morning."

"You are as energetic as I perceived from your writings. I am sure it's going to be great company for me as well."

"But first the gift!" As soon as she says that, she reaches out for her purse. Even as she opens her purse, I see the tag of 'Brighton' on it. I also recognise the brand by its signature leather work. It is feminine and elegant. Just like her!

"Here is a copy of my latest book. You may like to read it at leisure time," she says and hands over a copy of the book to me.

When I ask her for her signature, she takes out a Parker pen and writes her name in a beautiful cursive font.

"Here it is," she hands over the signed copy to me with a chuckle in her voice. I am becoming a little uncomfortable with the kind of adulation which I am receiving from a person who is far more accomplished than I am.

I thank her for the book and politely ask her for her choice of coffee. She wants to have cafe latte. I go to the counter and order two lattes. Then, I return, but not before picking up a few coffee beans that are kept on display. I also ask for a little bowl at the counter. This is not a usual demand from other customers at Starbucks, but they understand. After all, this is one thing I always ask for, every time I come to the café. The young and familiar guy at the counter smiles and hands over a little bowl with some roasted beans in it.

"Why these coffee beans?" she asks inquisitively as I reach the table.

"Well, I love breathing in the rich aroma of the coffee beans in all forms. I think there is a reason why Starbucks keeps these beans on display at a few places. This is called the complete Starbucks Coffee experience," I say, beaming with joy.

"Now I know that this conversation is going to be fun, somehow," she says excitedly.

"So let me come to the topic for today's meeting. I want to ask you a few questions about your transformation, Rohan."

"My transformation! I did not understand."

"See, I have read one of your interviews in which you talked about the lowest points of your life. You had mentioned about your struggling days but you did not give the details. Then, I saw some more stories on your social media page. They fascinated me, so I was hoping to know more about your life. You never know, they can become the chapters of an upcoming book," she says, in an encouraging tone.

"Hmm! This is going to be a long story. Are you willing to spend that much time?" I can hear the barista calling my name. Coffee is ready. I tell her, "Let me first get the coffee."

"Sir, whose names should I write on the mugs?" he asks.

"Analia on one mug. On the second mug, just make a smiley. No names. I make people smile and that is my identity," I say and smile at the barista. Then, I grab both the mugs and reach out for my table.

"Oh wow, this looks to be the perfect mug for today's interview,"

I settle and look at her.

"Thank you for showing interest in my story. I don't know whether you have read the interview wherein I had mentioned that phase in my life when I wanted to end my life. From then to now, it's a super thrilling story. No wonder my interviews caught your fancy. You are a journalist, after all! You can 'smell' great stories."

Analia looks at me intently and gives a serene smile.

"This story is in two parts. The first part begins from a hill station and ends in a dark room when I get a call. The second part begins from the same dark room with me getting a call and ends here in front of you. Are you ready for it?" I ask.

"Yes. You can also tell me about what you are doing now," she says as she punches a few words in her electronic notepad.

"Over the last many months, I have been doing two things. I have been busy expanding my business where I am setting up a fully integrated counselling business, pan India. I have a detailed list of cities where I will have my call centres placed in such a manner that people can get instant counselling and hand-holding in any language spoken in India. My vision is to create the world's largest relationship counselling and life transformation helpline network, which includes support in every possible language spoken on earth. I want to have a tie-up with health, wellness and yoga centres around the world. Our team has been receiving plenty of calls every month and we are providing instant guidance to people, thereby saving many lives and inspiring many people to transform their life." I can see Analia listening attentively.

"Can I record this conversation, if you don't mind? I have a few questions to ask. Then, I am planning to write articles in some of the most widely read journals and newspapers in the country. I want more people to know about your vision, passion and purpose."

I agree to her request. Analia begins recording in her iPhone voice memo. After two hours of an intense interactive session, Analia is done with today's interview. She is reflecting intently on our conversation.

"Rohan! Please take my advice. You must write a book on the journey of your transformation. I will help you with the editing and publishing. I will also support you with the marketing. I know for sure that your book deserves to be read by millions of youth in this country. I am mesmerised with the kind of defining experiences that you just narrated to me. Your story could become the guiding light for anyone who is struggling to make sense of their dark circumstances."

"Are you serious?" I say with a bit of surprise.

"Yes. Apart from being a journalist, I am also an author. Based on what I've gathered from your narration, you have the stuff for a bestseller. In fact, your book is the perfect 'Breakup Bible' which everyone who has experienced heartbreak must read." She sounds more confident than me on the latent potential of a book.

"Breakup Bible – this is the best term one can give to my story. Thank you for saying that," I say as we both get up.

♋

The sun has set and it is a nice and breezy evening. The whole sky has turned orange and the gulmohar tree is full of chirping birds. The sound is soothing as the rhythm of their song fills my heart with immense joy and hope.

Analia can see that I am lost in my thoughts as we wait for the driver to bring our car.

"I guess you have decided the name of the book," she says and laughs.

"To be honest, you have set me thinking. And I guess, I can also tell you the name of the book," I say as I see our cars coming.

"That is awesome. What is it? I knew your story would make a perfect bestselling book. Finding the name would not be difficult. But still, I did not know that you would find the name so fast," she says and rushes to the driving seat after grabbing the key from the driver.

"So what is the name?" she asks as she lowers the window of the car on my side.

*"My Twisted Love Story,"* I say while still being lost in my thoughts.

♋

I begin to write my story from the very next day.

Initially, it is pretty challenging to think where to start the story from. But, I just take one chapter at a time. I pen down my experiences spontaneously.

Soon, I compose long paragraphs and then chapters begin to unfold. The more I write, the more excited I get to see how the story is taking shape. It's as if Newton's law of inertia is working.

Till I hadn't started writing, I thought I could never write. But when I did, I started getting more clarity about what my narrative is going to look like. Newton was right – things in motion tend to stay in that state unless an external force stops it. I got into the flow of writing, and interestingly, there is no external force capable of stopping me now.

*Am I the same man who wanted to end everything in life till that phone call came?* I am left wondering.

Days become weeks and weeks become months. Soon, the story of my life begins to take final shape. The season has changed.

When I meet Analia next, it would be spring in Pune. Now, it is monsoon and my book is ready.

Let me read it out for you before it goes to Analia.

Ready for the stroll?

# 2

# A Walk through Dream Land

## Three years ago

*God is a great leveller.*
*He made life and he made death.*
*He made night and then he made the day.*
*He made pain and he made joys.*
*He made fire and he made water.*
*He made tall mountains and deep seas.*
*He made dullness and he made the feeling of exhilaration.*
*He made failures and then he designed success.*
*He made ignorance and he made enlightenment.*
*He made men and he also made women.*
*He made the 'real world of struggle' and a 'dreamlike world of love'.*
*He made the teachers who punished me every time I struggled to understand their questions.*

*He also made the girl, looking into whose eyes made me forget all the punishments and failures.*
*God made the teachers who never saw anything great in me.*
*He also made her who saw my talents of poetry and paintings and appreciated these every time we met.*

"Rohan, you are a romantic person. You will fall in love many times. But, falling out of love will be a silent and painful journey for you." Rajan had told me this a few times.

He was known to be one of the wisest students in college where I had taken admission three years ago.

"And why do you think so?" I could not resist asking him when he said this again today.

"Hey, I know the psychology of people. It's easy for you to fall in love. You will do this again and again." Rajan was quite amused to see me perplexed.

I still could not understand how someone could make such a confident assertion without knowing me completely. After all, he had known me only for the last few months after we met in the hostel. Everyone knew him since he was the topper of the class. Unlike him, who was fairly popular among the girls of the college, I was an average student with decent looks whom nobody feels like giving a second look to. Just like the protagonist in the movie *Hollow Man* who nobody could take a note of.

I was still wondering how someone else knew me better than I knew myself! It's true that others can see us better whereas we need a mirror to see even our face. I was grasping the initial difference, I guess.

The conversation happened when I had just told Rajan about my feelings for a girl in the college. I was not sure whether it was love or just infatuation, and hence wanted to have the 'wise man's advice'. The day I first saw her, I knew that there was something unique about her. Something about her attracted me with a compelling force, but I could never explain. It was as real, powerful and invisible as the law of gravity. Nobody can see the gravitational force, but we all feel it.

I still remember my feelings when I saw her first. When I set eyes on her for the first time, she was talking to some friends. Since I had always been shy, I was trying to look into her eyes sheepishly. I did not want anyone to catch me staring at her. I was mesmerized with everything about her. Her eyes were incredibly beautiful. Her hair was long and dark, her brows arched subtly and her eyes were deep enough for me to drown into them. I loved the way she tossed her hair back from her ever-pink cheeks. Her smile captured all my attention and the grace with which she walked could startle anyone. She was always surrounded by her friends. Due to her captivating personality, she was the centre of attraction. She was like the sun around which all her friends revolved like planets. Or maybe only I could visualise this celestial arrangement. Was it really the truth or the love that I felt for her?

Slowly, I realised that this is how love changes your perception and takes you to a world of dreams and fantasies.

I did not know then that soon, I will also become one of the planets, the nearest one, and revolve around her, day and night.

In my childhood days, I was passionate about making paintings. I used to love making a rainbow in the sky. My love was so intense that sometimes, I would even paint multiple rainbows in the sky. I loved colours. Anything in this world which made me use all the colours was close to my heart. I never knew then that there will come a time in my life when the rainbows will descend on the horizon of my life itself. The rainbows will have the colours of love and separation. I did not know then that my life was going to become a sky with multiple rainbows of different colours and emotions!

That was another reason I fell in love with her. She also loved colours. No wonder when I saw her in the same college where I studied, my joy knew no bounds.

Apart from painting, I had another talent since my childhood days, which was lying dormant till now. I didn't know back then that this 'hidden talent' would grow and envelope my life like never before. It was my creative bent to write poems.

When I got mesmerised by her beauty and charm, I started writing poems and since I was head over heels in love with her, I shared these poems with her – first over WhatsApp and then through letters. I still don't know what transpired in her mind, but she started encouraging me to write more poems. I used to recite the poems while sitting in front of her on a bench near the riverside. There were just too many students in college and hence we often used to drive to the nearby riverside and sit on a bench in an area where not too many people visited.

You might be thinking that it was a cakewalk for me. Let me rephrase my journey of love so far. The days of us meeting on the riverside came after months of writing poems for her and sharing colourful paintings dedicated to her beauty. One thing led to another and we became close friends. There came a day when I proposed to her through a letter. She neither accepted nor rejected my proposal.

I was scared for the next few days, thinking about her reaction to my letter. But, I used to see her smiling more often while talking to me after that day. She showcased some anger, but I knew that this anger was as transient as the dewdrops in early morning summer sun. I mean, somehow I knew this anger was only a façade behind which I could see her smile and affection for me.

After meeting her, I began to see all the colours of the rainbow in her personality. After being in love with her, I noticed that even emotions had a colour to them. I went through so many emotions when I was with her that I could literally allocate a colour to each of them. Colours from my childhood rainbows had changed their meaning for me.

My whole world had shrunk within her thoughts. She became the universe for me. Or, I think, she was the Sun and I became her Mercury, the closest planet to her. There were other guys roaming around her, but I was the lucky one, being the closest in the warmth of her love. At least that is what I thought.

*Was I blinded in love? I was not sure then; but today, I know I was. Completely!*

♋

It was her birthday and I wanted to make it the best experience for her. I had started thinking and planning for her special day a month in advance. I was thinking of how to make this birthday the best memory of her life.

While walking in the morning, I thought of how to surprise her with my wish. I was wondering about the time when I should wish her.

*Should I wish her at midnight like most of the people do or should I wish her a day before anyone else could think of wishing her? Which gift should I give her?*

I had to ensure that my gift was unique. Even the thought of making her happy gave me thrills. I could visualise her smiling face, her beautiful eyes, the pink blush on her cheeks, her kind words of compliments and most importantly, the feeling of affection that she had for me. These thoughts were driving me to do anything that would make me the best lover in the world.

Now I know why god makes people experience love. Falling in love gives people a temporary sense of utopia. The same world which is often filled with pain, misery, drudgery and broken dreams becomes the perfect place when you are with the right person. God knows well that the world he has created is imperfect. Hence, he created the spirit of love to make this imperfect world appear *more than perfect*.

I had been experiencing a strange but sweet change in my thoughts and feelings. I had started seeing a new meaning in little things of life. Earlier, a drive to some place was an impatient wait to reach the destination. But now, the drive was the most beautiful part of the journey.

If I drove along with her, the drive became more intoxicating than the joys of reaching the destination. What pleasure I derived while just feeling her presence in the car as I travelled through beautiful hills and green countryside. I often held her fingers in mine and she always got angry, asking me to focus on driving. She smiled and blushed as she knew I was head over heels in love with her. I knew that she loved the feeling, no matter what she said.

These little moments of driving with her used to be my most memorable and celebrated moments. She loved my little gestures of keeping her favourite chocolates in the car on her side of the dashboard cabinet. On seeing those, she used to exclaim in happiness and my joy knew no bounds. For the first time, I knew the true meaning of a joyride. It was my father's car, which he had asked me to keep in the new town where my college was located.

Often while driving through a lonely and beautiful road, I used to stop the car and we both got down. We stood there taking support of the side of the car, looking at the hills and countryside on the horizon. I had written a poem for her and read the poem while gazing where the hills met the horizon. I saw a twinkle in her eyes when she heard it. Her smiles used to be wider, blush on her face shinier and her eyes dreamier when she heard my poems. I used to look at her face and often deep into her eyes – to see if she was also looking at me instead of looking into the horizon.

♋

I still remember that drive, which became the most beautiful experience of my life. We stopped on the way to have a nice lunch. It was a restaurant by the side of the road. I had come to the place earlier as well, but today the place seemed to be straight out of the world of dreams.

You see things around you based on what you think and imagine. I was lovelorn that day and hence my eyes caught the glimpse of a garden adjacent to the restaurant. It was an open-air restaurant adjoining a garden, which did not matter to me earlier when I came to the same place along with my college friends. But today, the same garden looked like 'the place to go to'. I asked her if she would join me for a walk after a nice lunch and she agreed.

We had a romantic walk in the garden. There were flowery trees and a lush green lawn. There was a small fountain too. The puddle of water, which was supposed to be a pool but did not seem to get any care from the gardener, if there was one at all, was not very clean. But, due to the sweet company, even the puddle appeared to be better than Dal Lake in Kashmir to me. And the fountain looked more beautiful than the famous one from Mysore garden.

The walk along with her in that garden was like a dream come true for me. We just walked and talked for hours. For me, as she giggled at something that I said, my heart became a butterfly. As she smiled while looking into my eyes, the grass beneath my feet became as soft as clouds. I was walking amidst the clouds. She, in her white suit, looked like a fairy that day. I also noticed that on that day, she wore a little black *bindi* on her forehead which I had never seen her wearing earlier.

*Was she wearing it today only for me?* She certainly looked more beautiful today.

*Did she also want to impress me, just like I had done everything possible to make her feel special on that day*?

The time just flew till I heard the honking of our car. The chauffeur must be getting restless while waiting. It was afternoon and we had to leave, though I did not want to leave the garden.

After an hour, we reached her place. I gifted her favourite book, chocolates and a bouquet. She loved them and gave me a warm hug. My heart was left behind with her. It seemed to be caught in the last few flaps of her eyelashes as she bid me goodbye in the sweetest voice. A journey of dreams had come to an end!

As I returned from her house to the railway station from where I was to catch an overnight train, her thoughts engulfed me.

My happiness turned into the pain of separation. I was trying to sleep on my berth, but my restless heart had no cure. Somehow, my heart was telling me that this 'walk through the clouds' was about to come to an end and this relationship was not going anywhere. We were from different family backgrounds, speaking different languages, coming from different states and having different cultures.

I lay there, enduring my emotionally turbulent state throughout the train journey.

# 3

## The Valley of Tears

My heart had started beating fast and my knees seemed to lose their strength. My legs were trembling but I did not even care for them. I was not even able to breathe now. I felt a pain in my chest. The pain was unbearable.

Ever since she had walked out of my life, I did not know when I ate, slept, walked and sat comfortably. All I felt was intense loneliness, which seemed to be killing me. The unflinching pain was searing through my heart and mind.

The moment I switched off the lights, her face began to shine in front of my eyes in the darkness. If I kept my eyes open, I saw her face floating over me. I heard her voice which once used to take my breath away. Her sweet voice, which used to make my heart skip a beat in earlier days, reminded me of an irreparable loss.

*If you want to understand love, just think of a river of fire which you have to cross while being fully submerged.*

I used to wonder what the famous poet really meant by comparing love with such a traumatic and painful experience. I could never get the meaning till I was in love myself. My days and nights were like a dreamland and this poem would never have meant anything for me.

Then, one day, I lost her from the world of my love and my life changed forever. I knew that if love was like a river of fire, I was at the deepest. Half of the journey was still left to cover and I was already losing my battle with life. But hold on, if the same poem is true, then it also means that there is an end to this journey of pain and misery. I just need to bear with this pain for a little more time.

For the time being, my heart was beating fast and my legs were shaking. I had to hold on to the grills of the window to save myself from falling. I was holding onto them and breathing heavily. But why did I feel this pain now?

That was because I saw *her* walking away with a handsome guy on the road behind the house that I was put up in during my week-long stay in the town. She lived in the neighbouring society and I had to face the moment I had been trying to avoid all these months. I did not want to see her again with another boy. But today, when I heard a familiar sound of giggles, I came to the rear window of the room to peep onto the road passing beside it. My legs were moving slowly towards the window and I was praying in my heart that it was not her.

Nevertheless, it was *her* voice. The same voice which I had yearned for till a year ago.

As I moved a little further, my worst fears came true. She was talking to a young and handsome boy. She was sitting on the front seat and the boy was holding her fingers while sitting on the rear seat. He was apparently teaching her how to ride a scooty. Both of them were enjoying the ride and were giggling and laughing together. Looked like the new guy in her life did not only study in the same college, but also lived near her house!

I saw her bright face clearly and then the old memories came alive again. I could not hold on to the grills of the window any longer and slowly collapsed along the wall onto the floor of the room. My pain gave way to cries and I began to weep inconsolably. I did not know how long I cried before slumping on the floor and falling asleep there.

When I woke up, it was dark all around me. I remembered the sight which had made me collapse on the ground. I was again feeling the same intensity of pain.

*What should I do? Is there any end to my misery?*

♋

So, how did my life change after my last drive to her hometown?

After my overnight train journey, I reached my hometown. Within a week of reaching there, my mother fell ill. She was diagnosed with a rare medical heart condition which meant that she had very little life left. My mother needed care at all times and my father fell into depression, seeing his life partner losing the battle of life. My father had his whole life revolving around his family and his social life was to the bare minimum. In his helplessness to see his life partner drifting away from the shore of life – the same partner with whom he had dreamt of spending his old age times, as he had none other than her to share his everyday stories – he also started showing early signs of memory loss. He had a running business so I had to be with both my parents to support them through this difficult time.

I decided to take admission in a local college in my native town. I looked after my parents and my family business. It was a heart-breaking decision for me as I knew that I was getting away from the girl who had made my life beautiful in the last few months.

I tried to communicate more often by sharing my poems to reclaim her love and compensate for our physical distance. But somehow, times had changed. Her messages became shorter. In fact, they became rare with time. I was told by one of my friends from the old college that she had started going out with another guy in my college. He was more handsome than I was. He was a better student than I was. Maybe he did not shower more love than I did, but she might have compromised with these little 'sweet nothings' as it did not matter to her anymore.

*Eventually, I had lost the race of love. She had moved past me, holding someone else's hand.*

♋

My mother passed away after a few months despite medical support and care. These were the toughest times for my family.

After a fortnight of doing her last rites, I decided to visit the town in which my ex girlfriend lived. I wanted to see if I could rekindle our spark. I went and stayed with one of my friends whose house was in the same locality in which she lived. I wanted to meet her.

And then the 'scooty incident' happened, which shattered my heart. Later, I came to know that she was head over heels in love with the guy I had seen her with. She did not respond to my messages despite knowing that I was in the vicinity after so long. It was all over between us.

I had been living in the pain of separation from her over the last couple of months. There had not been a single day when I did not miss her. On certain evenings, I used to make repeated calls, just to hear her voice. On other evenings, I used to send my little poems to her.

But nothing was working now. I got more and more desperate. After my mother's death, I was immersed in limitless sadness and a sense of loss.

It had been tough for me for many months. I could not take it anymore. So, I reached out for my phone. I opened the google app and typed – *Painless way of death.*

I saw numerous search results. The time had come to get rid of these miserable days and nights. I opened one of the links and read it. I started going through the links one by one. I could feel the taste of tears at the edges of my lips. I did not even know when the tears dried up while rolling down my cheeks and leaving a trail on both sides of my lips down till they met in the chin.

I got a sense of déjà vu. I could recollect that I had felt the same saline taste on my lips while wiping someone else's dried up tears.

♋

It was Valentine's Day when I had taken her for a ride on the outskirts of the city. We had a lovely drive and lunch in a restaurant beside a road passing through a hilly terrain. The city had beautiful weekend getaways and there was no dearth of romantic places nestled in the lap of hills.

In the valley, there was a beautiful restaurant which had the best of both worlds – a roadside *dhaba* feel and an upmarket five-star hotel ambience. It was in this restaurant where I had booked a table which was overlooking the lake. She was mesmerised to be in such a romantic place where we had come to celebrate the day of love. I had also planned a surprise for her. As she looked at the blue water of the lake and the reflection of mountains in the water, I stood behind her and recited the poem, my hand on her delicate shoulders. My left-hand fingers played with her shoulder and neck. I could feel that she was getting moved by the soulful rendition of the most enchanting poem I had ever written.

I felt a few drops of warm tears falling on my fingers.

*Was she crying? Was she moved with my words?*

I finished reading the last line of the poem and came forward to look at her. I leaned forward, kept my hands on the table and looked at her face. She also turned her gaze towards me. Her eyes were overflowing with tears. Her lips were quivering and her cheeks had turned pink. She looked innocent, delicate and dreamlike beautiful. In that moment, she appeared to me like a fairy from heaven.

I was lost in her dark brown eyes when I saw her lips moving. I did not even realise when she had held my fingers with her hands.

"This is the most touching poem I have ever heard. You write so beautifully. I cannot believe *you* have written it. I am so lucky to receive so much love from you. This is the most memorable moment of my life." Her lips moved even as her tears made her lips wet from both sides.

I moved my face forward and locked her lips with mine. For the first time, I felt the saline taste of her tears.

♋

*Today, I had the same saline taste on the core of my lips. The taste was that of my own tears this time. This was going to be the last taste of my life!*

My life had changed so drastically. I knew my heart could not take this pain even for a moment now. I had received my share of love. It was time for me to end all of this.

I looked at my phone once again. So which was the most painless way of death? I could not read clearly as my eyes were full of tears by now. With my hands trembling, I reached out to the curtains in the windows in a desperate bid to look for something to wipe out my tears.

Then, I stared at the curtains for a while. They seemed to serve the purpose. The same curtains which were my windows to the world appeared to be the tool through which I could bring the curtains down on the story of my life forever. I took them off from the window and started tying them off together. With the rope in my hand, I knew what to do next.

It was exactly at this time that I heard my phone ringing. I did not take the call, but the phone kept ringing. It was from an unknown number.

*Who is this person?*

I got up, washed my face at the wash basin, dried my face with a towel and went to the phone.

And the rest, as they say, is history.

# 4

## *The Last Game*

"Hey Rohan, Jayesh here. It has been many years since we spoke. I don't know if you remember me. Do you…?" It was a crisp voice at the other end.

My energy was hitting rock bottom but as I could make from the voice on the other side, the caller's energy was skyrocketing. Once upon a time, I also had the same vigour in my voice. That's until I fell out of love.

"Jayesh, yes! I remember you. How are you doing?" I mumbled in a feeble voice.

"Hey Rohan, what happened to you? Are you fine?" It is surprising how people can read one's mind even while speaking over phone from hundreds of miles away.

"I thought you would jump with joy on hearing from your old friend," his exuberance was getting on my nerves as this appeared to be a call at the wrong time.

"This is too much Jayesh. You never cared for my well-being all these years. You are calling me after ages and now you are so concerned about me," I said in a dispassionate tone. There was a silence from the other side for a while.

"Sorry Rohan. But I am worried after hearing your emotionless voice," he said. "You were not like this. What has happened?"

"Nothing Jayesh. Life has been good and it is moving well to its destination," I murmured. I was surprised at my newfound 'cold confidence', as I would like to call it.

"Rohan, I am talking to you after so many years and you are still so serious. Come on! Don't take life so seriously! And see, at least I called you, but you have completely forgotten me. You also could have thought of calling me. I was talking to Muthu the other day, the same nerd who was with us in the college. He also complained of not having heard from you for ages." Jayesh was trying his best to make the conversation livelier. I think he had gauged my sombre mood from my lacklustre and dead voice.

"So tell me, how did you remember me?" I asked. Jayesh must have understood that I was not interested in taking this conversation any further.

"Look Rohan, I have got great news for you. This is as if you are going to win a lottery. Don't you want to know more about this?" I heard Jayesh and could almost imagine him smiling on the other side.

"I don't want any lottery. You can keep it on my behalf," I mumbled without a trace of excitement in my voice.

"Hey Rohan! What happened? You seem to be very upset man!" Jayesh seemed hurt by my monotonous replies.

His condition was like someone who was blowing into a bonfire which was doused long ago, expecting some sparks hidden beneath the heap of ash, but finding none. I was feeling bad for him. There was silence at both ends for some time. Finally, I blinked and my silent trance broke.

"Jayesh, I am sorry but I am going through a really bad phase of life. In fact, I have lost interest in life. To cut the story short, I was in love with a girl and we had a breakup a few months ago. It has been really bad for me ever since. It's long since we spoke last. And most importantly, I lost my mother recently, so I am at a very dark place right now. I am sorry to tell you this, but I don't want to live anymore." Tears, which had welled up in the core of my eyes, had started choking my voice by the time I finished speaking.

I was shocked at how I had disclosed all of this to an old friend with whom I hadn't even been in active touch. Maybe, I was on the brink of an emotional collapse and needed someone to hear me out. And since I got a shoulder to cry on, I just caved in.

"Rohan, I am so happy that you told me. This shows that our trust is still intact, even after so many years. My life lessons have proven beyond doubt that our whole life can change if we share our story with the right person. I can say with humility that you have shared this issue with the *right* person.

"I am a life coach and a motivational speaker. I know what you are going through. No amount of preaching is going to help you. Unless you get the strength to change the course of your life, nothing favourable will happen. But, before that, let me give you the news," Jayesh took a pause, as if to assess whether I was listening.

After being reassured that I was there, he said, "I never told you in all these years, but I owe some money to you. You are going to be richer by one-and-half lakh rupees. This is like a lottery, as you did not know about this," he said. I was taken aback, honestly. I didn't know what he was talking about.

He must have understood my silence, because he quickly added, "Let me explain. You remember, I had visited your house during Diwali vacation many years ago. We were studying together and were living in the same hostel. During that stay, while talking to your dad, I had told him about my intention to study in a MBA college. I also told him that I won't be able to join the MBA institute due to shortage of money. He did not know that I had lost both my parents, and somehow I had continued my education until college while getting support from my brother-in-law. But the admission fee for my dream MBA college was far too high. I couldn't even think of asking for sponsorship from my sister and brother-in-law.

"Your dad generously offered to sponsor the study fee of the college before I left your home. For some strange reason, he asked me not to reveal this to you. Later he told me that you had sent the money to him for his medical treatment and you would not let him use it for any other reason. Hence, he wanted this to be kept a secret from you. Now I am working in a multi-national company and its time to return the money. I spoke with your father yesterday. Surprisingly, this time he himself told me to inform you about this. He thought for a while and asked me to return the money to you. And I am so glad that he advised me so. I think you needed to talk to someone and I think you cannot have anyone better than me. It's my passion to help people transform their life." Finishing thus, Jayesh went silent for some time.

"This is great news to me. I am so happy that my father helped you. But that said, I don't know what to do with my life. What will I do with the money now?" I stopped to hold my tears back.

"Look, Rohan! I know that to say that you are unhappy with life would be an understatement. I did not know that our conversation will take this turn but now, I am going to say something which is even more surprising to you than the lottery thing." I could hear a hint of excitement in Jayesh's voice.

"Now what is that? You are dropping bombs after bombs today Jayesh!" I said restlessly. I was surprised to find that after having been in conversation with Jayesh over some time, I was feeling lighter and slightly better.

This is an interesting fact of this world. When our mind gets occupied with a negative thought, it will get sucked into an ever-expanding pool of negativity. One negative thought attracts more negative thoughts. Just like when we first light one candle and then use the same to light other candles in sequence. It reminds me of the game of dominos which we used to play in our childhood days. While playing, we either arranged the bricks in a straight line or kept them in a curvilinear pattern. Whichever way we organised the bricks, once we pushed one brick, other bricks also fell one after the other until the last brick collapsed. The only way to break the chain of negativity is to cause a break in the pattern. In the game of dominos, which we played with bricks in our childhood days, we could easily stop the fall by keeping an intermediate brick away from the adjacent one.

I was in a web of negativity and this call from Jayesh was that perfect break – the increased distance between two bricks which had broken the trend of further falling of the bricks. In other words, his call had *changed* the pattern of my thinking.

*What would have happened had he not called me?* I still would have been lost in the energy-draining thoughts about my love life.

"Hey dude, what happened? You are silent. Don't you want to hear about the game of life which I am going to discuss with you?" Jayesh chuckled at the other end. He might have been scared and concerned at my silence.

"Oh yes, Jayesh. I am all for it. Somehow I am getting the feeling that this call from you seems to be the best thing to have happened to me in last many months. Thanks buddy," I said with my voice choked with emotions again.

"Look dude, first things first – you need to be kinder to yourself. Have you not seen the powerful talks by Muniba Mazari on YouTube? She is an activist and motivational speaker. You should see how she encourages people to be kind and compassionate, not only to others, but to themselves as well. What you went through is a difficult experience and nothing more than that. Life is a collection of diverse experiences – both sweet and sour. Every experience is significant. There is a profound meaning in every life event that we go through," Jayesh said.

"Hey Jayesh, don't lecture me. These motivational blogs and talks do not take away the pain of suffering in real life." Jayesh understood that I was not impressed at all with what he had 'preached' to me.

"Now, you have challenged me, dude. This is the field of my passion. Before I talk about the game of life, I would like to show you how the message of motivational videos is absolutely correct." Jayesh paused for a while before resuming.

"Can you please think of one unhappy life moment from your past? I mean, you can think of the second worst thing after your breakup," Jayesh said in a serious tone.

I thought a bit before speaking up, "Hey let's leave it here and move on to the game thing that you spoke about. I mean, are you sure that you want me to think of another sad thing in my life? I am already a wreck as you may have realised by now." I wanted to dodge this discussion.

"It would be fun. I am telling you. Just think of one past life incident and narrate it briefly. Then, we will see how it gets connected to your life in a meaningful way." I could sense that Jayesh was in no mood to relent.

"The next painful memory which I can think of is when I failed in my ninth grade examination. You know I am not very good in studies. But failing in an examination and wasting a year was something I had never imagined. That was really difficult. Though it happened many years ago, I still feel sad," I said while thinking.

"Rohan, life is a matter of how you look at things. I will say – that was the best moment in your life. When Mahatma Gandhi was forced to move out of the first-class compartment of the train at Pietermaritzburg Railway station, he felt deeply humiliated. But that one bitter experience also gave him a life-changing realisation which made him a *mahatma*. Had this unpleasant incident not taken place in his life, he would have remained Mohandas Gandhi, a person who always wanted to dress, speak and look like the British. He received the motivation to change the mindset of people who discriminated with people based on their colour from this painful incident. Mohandas got the purpose of his life."

"You are right. This is an interesting thought. But what has it got to do with my failure in ninth grade?" I asked with a bit of surprise.

"If you look at them carefully, both the situations are similar. Mohandas Gandhi wanted to travel in the first-class compartment to achieve respect and equality in life, but he was thrown out of that place. You also wanted to travel in the 'compartment of respect' through academic success, but were unsuccessful. Both the cases are of rejection and humiliation. Both the cases are of not reaching the destination. But ultimately, just like Mahatma Gandhi became a great man after accepting his circumstances and initiating his journey of transformation, you should also rise to the challenge. This moment of disappointment was the Universe's way of telling you that you needed to make some change in your life.

"Now you tell me, did you not start taking your academics more seriously after that incident? Did you not study harder after that transformational event? Hence, that incident had an important role to play in your life. That is what I mean when I speak about connecting the dots by looking back in time." Jayesh smiled and paused.

"Awesome man! I am happy to know such a different perspective. I never thought of that episode in this way. But what about the game?" I asked.

"Coming to the game. Listen to me carefully. I know you do not want money. You are unhappy with your life. I will design a game of life for you. In this game, I will arrange for you to travel to five places in the country. I will make all the travel and accommodation arrangements. I am a professional life coach and I am doing this for a reason. You may not understand the purpose now, but you can connect the dots later on. You can say that the money which I owe you will be used to plan this game of life for you. The money will give you an incredible experience of your lifetime.

"*Life is beautiful*, says the title of the Oscar-winning movie by Roberto Benigni. I realised it after being on the path of my self-transformation and life coaching. Now it's your turn to appreciate life. Like every game, this game will also be full of surprises. You will play it step by step. I will send you the clue of one destination at a time. You have to visit the place and spend some time there. At each place, you will get the clue for the next destination. The game will go on till you visit all the five places. Then I will have a chat with you and we will connect the dots. Your visit to each of these places will be transformative, I can assure you of that. So, are you ready for the game?" Jayesh asked me.

"Yes, I am. It is for the first time in the last few months that I am feeling excited. I am ready for this game of life..." I said, though I was still a bit unsure of what waited ahead.

"Awesome man! So you will get the first clue by today evening. You will get a WhatsApp message with your destination and e-tickets. All the best," said Jayesh before ending the call with a smile.

♋

As per Jayesh's message, I was supposed to meet Mr Mehta in Mumbai. Jayesh had sent me the tickets of an inter-city Uber cab. I had to catch the cab after three days. Then, I had to spend a day with Mr Mehta in Mumbai. My accommodation was booked in a hotel facing Nariman Point.

*Not a bad arrangement to begin the game of life!* I thought.

'The Last Game' was to begin from Pune, my hometown.

# 5

## Count Your Blessings

"Welcome Mr Rohan, you are going to have a life-changing experience today. You will never regret any moment of your life henceforth, probably even the ones you never wanted to live. You will thank god for every moment which will come your way," Mr Mehta said without blinking his eyes.

I just followed him as he walked, all the while wondering if I was with a guy who made pre-mature judgements and loved preaching all the time.

He had come to pick me up from the hotel where Jayesh had arranged for my accommodation. He was my local guide who was supposed to take me to my first destination.

When we drove off from the hotel in an Innova, little did I know that my game of life will begin from a narrow lane in *aamchi Mumbai*.

We got down from the car on a busy road in the heart of Mumbai and were walking towards another part of the city which looked even more congested and unkempt. The road on which we were moving in Mr Mehta's car was full of pedestrians, animals, hawkers, motor bikes and city transport buses which were jostling with each other to make headway in their struggle of reaching their destinations.

The sun was shining in its full glory and I could see people perspiring in the sweltering Mumbai heat. However, we were comfortably placed in the cosy confines of the air-conditioned car. Two diametrically opposite worlds existed in that very space.

I recalled the sayings of my father when we were young. He always used to tell me and my brother.

"Look, there are always two sides of the same coin. Day and night, love and loss, hope and despair, energy and lethargy, good and bad, Ram and Ravana. We all have two sides within us – the good and the bad. The bright and the dark. You have to be careful enough to let the brighter side take over. Always do good deeds and keep away from bad actions." I also recalled how amused we used to be while hearing him say all these words. I never understood the depth of his words back then.

I often asked him, "But Papa, how come this is true? How can good and bad be within us? We are either good or bad. We cannot be both. Look at my classmates. Some are good and others are bad. Ramesh is always so kind to me and Prasanna is always being naughty to other students in the classroom."

To that, my father replied, "Son, all that I have learnt in life is that good people are half-bad and bad people are half-good. Just as sunrise and sunset are a part of the same world that we live in, we have the elements of good and bad within us. It is up to us to let the good shine and the bad disappear. If we do not think of good thoughts and practise good habits, we will be surrounded by negativity. For example, if you do not build the habit of waking up early in the morning, you will be habituated to wake up late. If you do not study hard, you will grow up into an ignorant youth. If you do not exercise, you will become a lazy boy. You have to consciously build a good life or else you will unconsciously be forced to live a mediocre life."

I still did not understand what he said. When I went to the college, the words of Ella Wilcox left a lasting impact in my life.

*There are two kinds of people on earth today,*
*Two kinds of people no more I say.*
*Not the good or the bad, for it's well understood,*
*The good are the half bad, the bad are half good.*

Ella explained how the masses in the world could not be classified into the neat categories of rich and poor. Apparently, rich people might be poor in health and might lack in conscience. However, she believes that people can be categorized into 'leaners' and 'lifters'. Lifters uplift the energy and spirit of people, and the leaners, as one can make out, let others bear their share of sorrow.

In short, lifters *will alleviate others' pain* by taking a part of their worries, and leaners *will increase others' burden* by passing on their pain to others.

I had been a leaner so far.

*Can I change positively to become a lifter? Can I become the pillar on which others could rely?*

While I was lost in thought, Mr Mehta stared at my brooding face.

"Mr Rohan, now we are about to enter the place which is going to be an incredible experience for you," Mr Mehta said when he saw me smiling.

"Oh yes, Mr Mehta. I am looking forward to this journey," I said as if I was woken up from a deep slumber.

"By the way, how far away is the destination?" I was speaking frequently now, as if to hide my embarrassment of being lost in my own world over the last few minutes. Perhaps, he might have guessed it by my long silence.

"Well it is here. Right at this place." He stopped the car with a screeching sound.

I was surprised. I could not see anything special there. I thought I was being taken to one of those luxurious places in the southern part of Mumbai. But here we were! Beside a dirty nallah and an old and dilapidated hut with a thatched roof. There were poor children playing around us. I could feel the foul smell of stagnant drainage water. The road on which we had stopped the car had potholes, which must be getting filled with dirty water in rainy season.

"Let's get down, Mr Rohan. I will look for a parking space and then we will go to a place which will make you believe in the presence of divinity in this world."

I got down from the car. Mr Mehta drove to almost hundred metres ahead to find some safe space beside the road for parking the car.

I stayed where I had gotten down. I was sizing the place up till Mr Mehta came back. There was a little temple beneath an old banyan tree besides the road. Some people were sitting on the thick roots of the banyan tree. There were few hutments around the temple and it was difficult to see the huts being separate from the temple. They all had merged and grown together, it seemed.

The spirit of human survival in the lap of nature!

"What are you looking at, Mr Rohan? The old temple? Come, I will take you to a place which does not have any temple but has faith written all around it. The place will make you believe in the beauty of life. I know that you have not been happy for some reasons in the last few months. Now, it's time to change the way we look at our existence." I was getting a bit amused.

*What did he mean? How can I see the beauty of life in such a dirty place? This is a place which I did not even know existed in the same bustling city of skyscrapers and towering buildings. I never knew that the same city of dreams also had a stinking lane where I would never have come had Mr Mehta not pulled me in his car.*

We started walking. With each step, I saw that our path was becoming narrower. First, the road became a walkway and the walkway a footpath. By the time we came to the end of the road, it was nothing more than a heap of dirt and dust. It had houses with thatched roof on both sides.

"You must have heard of this place Mr Rohan. This is Dharavi. The largest slum in India, though it is located in a very small area of just 2.1 square kilometres. More than ten lakh people live here. As you can see, the living conditions are not very good here. A whole family lives in a 12 feet by 10 feet home. This is less than the area of terraces and kitchens in many houses. But, I will show you an even strange home. Come with me," Mr Mehta started walking again.

We saw a cemented narrow walkway which was hardly five feet wide. We were now walking one behind the other with me following Mr Mehta. It was a wet and slippery walkway, which was too narrow to be called a road. The walkway was surrounded by houses whose windows, if opened, could have hit one of us if we were not careful enough.

I was dumbstruck to see people living in such extreme poverty. It was not a small number as the population living there could have easily filled an entire township. There are so many people living in abject lack of basic amenities of life. I could never have realised this side of life, had I not come here.

Mr Mehta said, "I would like you to meet Mr Sangle and family. It's a family of six living in this pipe-cum-house for the last several years. When I invited the head of International Economic Forum for a visit to this place, she could not hold back her tears. Initially, she was filled with repulsion as I could clearly see the signs of abhorrence on her face. Then, the feeling of repulsion turned into a firm admiration for human endurance and spirit. After talking to the family for some time, she returned and on the way back, I saw tears welling up in her eyes. When asked, she said these were the tears of joy. She had seen an unprecedented love for life among people who had almost nothing to lose."

I still remember her exact words which she said to me.

"Mr Mehta, I have met some of the most celebrated people in the world. I have seen some of the richest people living under the fear of losing their opulence. I have seen people being so depressed despite living in huge palaces. But I was so touched to talk to the family members, who despite having nothing, are living so happily. They are close to each other and celebrate all the festivals together. If we want to learn the art of counting the blessings, these people whom we just met could be the best teachers. In fact, I am thinking of inviting them for one of our summits. I think we can get some inspiration from them."

I was hearing Mr Mehta while standing a little away from their house. Then, we met Mr Sangle and his family.

I was wondering if people who had more in life, complained more, and those who did not have much, whined less. This was against the conventional logic. After all, you expect people having less wanting more and hence complaining more frequently. Similarly, you also expect people having more to be less demanding and being happier with their life. But the reverse appeared to be true here!

"Mr Rohan, would you like to talk to the family and know their life better? If yes, you will have to sit in their home for some time," Mr Mehta said.

"Sure Mr Mehta, I would *love* to do that," I said. I was surprised at me using the word love in a completely new context this time. Initially, I had used this world plenty of times to convey my feelings in my love letters. I could see how my thoughts and perspectives were changing now.

"I kept my shoes aside and sat inside their home. I saw different portions of the hume pipe being used as a kitchen, living room and drawing room. It had an open terrace as well, which was on the other side of the hume-pipe.

"What made you come to Mumbai?" I asked the first question. "Don't you think, you can live in a much larger area and house if you go back to your village?"

"Sir, we do not have any source of income in our village. But here, we get a good source of livelihood. What we lack in space in this slum area, is compensated well by what we gain here," he said. Then, after a brief pause, he continued, "Sir is there anyone who has everything that they desire? If we only think of what we don't have, we will spend all our life in misery and pain. If we spend all our life thinking of what we have, then our happiness will only grow." I was surprised at what Mr Sangle said to me.

"You have very enriching thoughts. May I know about your background?" I was surprised.

"Well, I was a teacher in a village school. I used to teach village students," he said to me.

"Then what made you come to live in such a crowded and unliveable place?" I asked, while trying my best to suppress my wonderment.

"Sir, if you see closely, this entire world in which we live can also be construed as *unliveable*. If you only look at the criminals, the world does not seem to be an ideal place to live. But if you look at the shining sun, fragrant flowers, green gardens, blue sky, especially those people like you who care for the world, the same world will look more liveable. I get to teach many students in the local schools and receive a good salary. I have been saving and if you meet us after a few months, we would have shifted to a bigger home, which is getting ready for me and my family. Life is what we make of it."

"How many kids do you have and how do you care for their education?" I asked.

"I have four kids and they all are studying in local schools in different classes. My role as a teacher has been influencing their studies favourably. I motivate them constantly by telling them about inspiring people who, despite experiencing an abject lack of resources, kept on moving forward and excelled incredibly. I believe that such stories can play a key role in making my kids believe that they can also be more successful one day," My Sangle said with pride.

"I am sure that in the same slum, many other people might also be living who are not as noble as you. Alcoholics, drug addicts, people who are involved in fights, abuses and brawls. How do you keep your family separate from them?" I asked.

"There is a small school located at some distance from here. My kids go to the school during the day. In the evening,

I take my kids to the school. There is a banyan tree outside the school, which is a well lit area. There are some benches there. My kids study there and I do my extra office work.

"Oh, I forgot to tell you. I am working as an accountant in a local leather processing and export firm. So, I complete my work in the evening. By the time we come back home, it is almost ten in the night. My wife and two little kids sleep in the hume pipe. Rest of us sleep outside in adjacent areas. We lay our cots outside and use mosquito nets. Many of our neighbours also have been living like that. The only difference between them and us is that we will be shifting to a nearby *chawl* in the next few months."

He took a brief pause so that I could process the information. Then, he continued, "Sir, I have seen one thing. If you behave well with people and live a virtuous life, the world comes to help you. When I went to the bank for loan, they sent their people to do background verification. The bank person got a good feedback about my conduct and behaviour. This helped me. Goodness is a seed, which becomes a tree and gives shade to others. When others get benefited from your good deeds, they become your community. That is how you become a more successful and happy person," Mr Sangle said.

I was amazed to see the simplicity of the man who was speaking to me.

"I think, it's time to move out Mr Rohan," Mr Mehta said from a distance. He must have been wondering why I was taking so much interest in the life story of Mr Sangle in this congested slum area.

"Sure, Mr Mehta," I said. "Mr Sangle, it's time for me to leave. It was a pleasure to be with you and your family. I am sure when I meet you next time, you would have shifted to your new house," I said with a spark in my voice.

"Yes sir, I would be sending an invite on my house-warming ceremony. You must come. We are so happy you came to our place. I could not even offer you a cup of tea. But when you meet us next time, you cannot leave without having dinner with our family," Mr Sangle's voice was brimming with emotions.

"Keep progressing. Stay strong as you have been all these years," I said while bidding adieu to him.

On our way back in the car, I was lost in my thoughts.

*Life is all a matter of attitude. We can be sad despite having everything except that one thing we want, and we can be happy despite losing everything, except a few things we need.*

I fell in the first category. I had everything but got depressed after losing a girl in my life. Mr Sangle cherished his blessings. He had a lovely family. Giving them a better life was his only dream. I decided to learn from this powerful interaction and change my perspective towards my life.

"So, Mr Rohan. Hope you enjoyed your visit. Did you realise by the way that god lives here and around us every moment?" he asked with a grin on his face.

"Yes, Mr Mehta. I think god lives within us. The problem is that we don't realise his presence and power as we forget to look inwards. If Mr Sangle can find so much of happiness at this place, god resides within him. It cannot be anything other than the divinity within him which is driving him ahead in life. It has been a spiritual and surreal experience for me."

I was looking outside the windows from the comfort of the air-conditioned car. I was seeing the other world – the same hot, humid and dusty world. The good and the bad worlds reside under the same roof created by god. It all depends on our mindset and what we choose to believe in.

Today, I was thinking of my childhood days when we used to celebrate Durga Puja. It was the celebration of goddess Durga, who is known as the goddess of power and courage. I always noticed something while going to various *pandals* (temporary structures where idols of Durga are kept; these are decorated with colourful articles and lighting). All the idols had both goddess Durga and the demon king Mahishasur made out of the same clay. These idols used to be created in one frame. Mother Goddess, riding the lion, was killing the demon king riding the buffalo. One represented the good and the other symbolised evil. Both used to coexist in every pandal.

We need to realise that both bright and dark sides exist within all of us. It's important that we let the good outshine the bad. It is important that we become a lifter and not a leaner.

At the moment, I was a 'leaner'; and Jayesh, a 'lifter'.

I did not know when we reached the hotel. I thanked Mr Mehta for his courtesy, time and hospitality before bidding goodbye to him. I was loaded with emotions, ideas, thoughts, spiritual awakening and gratitude today.

Overall, it was an insightful beginning to the 'Game of Life'.

♋

I had hardly returned to my hotel room when I got a WhatsApp message from Jayesh.

*I am sure you have become more grateful for this beautiful life that you are living. Mr Mehta called me and told me, you liked the visit to the place. Believe me! This life is like a magical box. It has so much of wonderful memories and experiences to offer. Whenever you feel low, you should count your blessings which will certainly act as a ray of hope.*

*By the way, you will soon receive the air tickets from Mumbai to Dehradun. At Dehradun airport, you will find a car which will take you to a beautiful place beside a lake in the foothills of the Himalayas.*

*All the best for your second destination. Talk to you later!*

*Love,*
*Jayesh*

I saw the tickets. I had an early morning flight. It was time for me to pack my bags and have dinner. And then, I also had to write my blessings. All of a sudden, life had become so busy. I was certainly enjoying this game of life!

Initially, I had a tough time thinking of blessings, but soon, the words started flowing on my laptop on which I was typing the blessings. My father, my home, my job, my colourful experience, my friends, my health, my love for music, books, poems, the fresh air, the morning, the evening moon and the list goes on and on...

It is true. We see what we want to see.

"Thank you Jayesh, for opening my eyes," I said with a heart full of peace and contentment.

# 6

# The Monk

I got up early the next morning. I had never woken up so early in the last few months. To my surprise, instead of feeling tired, I felt refreshed.

*Was I again falling in love? Perhaps, with myself and my life this time?*

It was too early to say, but I was sure that my thoughts were changing drastically.

Life is all about discovering your 'why'. I left for the airport in anticipation of another thrilling experience. Will my visit to the next place give me the same excitement to leave my bed early every day? I was yet to find out.

I did not know when I slept in the plane. Landing announcement from the cabin crew woke me up. I got ready to unfasten my seat belt. I looked at the watch. It was 7:30 a.m. and a car was waiting outside the airport. I kept my luggage and sat in the rear seat.

"How long shall we take to reach the *ashram*?" I asked the chauffeur.

"Sir, it will take us four hours. You can catch up with some sleep. You might have woken up early today. I come to the airport frequently to receive guests and mostly they catch up with some sleep on their way to the ashram. Most of the visitors find it literally an *eye-opening* experience when they open their eyes after reaching the ashram.

"Their first expression when they wake up after reaching the ashram is 'What a beautiful place!' Now, you can take some rest if you want." The chauffer was smarter than he appeared from his attire and demeanour.

*Why do we take things and people on their face value?* I wondered.

I remembered my grandfather's advice, which he had conveyed to me when I was very young.

*"Rohan, you should learn to see what is not obvious. Great people develop a rare ability to see what is not visible to the eyes at the first look. Your real success will come when you learn to see the roots, which are invisible. Everyone can see a building but may neglect the importance of the foundation on which the building stands. Foundations, as you know, are hidden beneath the surface. Everyone saw the sun revolving around the earth. Only Galileo could actually* see *the earth revolving around the sun. How did he develop this insight? This is a mysterious secret you will have to unearth yourself. If you can do that, you will also transform the world, just like Galileo did. You have to*

*develop the same intellect, mindset and ability to challenge the traditional theory."*

I did not understand what he meant back then. But, perhaps, I was beginning to see the real meaning of it now.

"Oh, do you work for the ashram?" I asked the chauffeur inquisitively.

"Yes sir! Guruji started this ashram with a small hut. But that was many years ago. Now, there is a series of cottages where many guests love spending some of the most enlightening days of their life."

"Okay, this sounds great. I am also looking forward to a memorable time there," I said.

I started looking outside the windows. I could see the picturesque beauty in front of me. Dehradun is the nearest airport for some of the most gorgeous hill stations of India and is nestled in lower Himalayas. I was mesmerized by the view and soon I dozed off in the car.

♋

"Sir, we have arrived." I heard the driver saying. I got up and looked around.

I was stunned. I was in front of a cottage, behind which there was a lake with clear blue water. The driver had switched off the car engine. I came out and looked around. It was pin drop silence which was only interspersed by the sound of swaying leaves from nearby trees.

I stood beside the lake and saw many cottages along the lake, which seemed to be guarded by mountains from the other three sides. It was midday and there was a cool breeze playing with my hair, while the golden sun warmed me up from above.

I turned back to see the driver keeping my luggage inside the cottage.

"Now you take some rest. In case you need anything, please call on the housekeeping number. Lunch will be served in the dining hall beside the lake. Afterwards, you should meet Guruji in the afternoon at 3 p.m. See you, sir."

The driver pointed his fingers towards a larger cottage, which appeared to be in the dining hall.

♋

"Come, Jayesh has told me about you. I am happy that you have come all the way to spend some quality time at this place. You have come here as Rohan, but will return as Rohan 2.0. I mean, your name will remain the same, but your thoughts and worldview will transform radically. You will have a new perspective of life."

Guruji said smilingly as I entered the hall where he was sitting on the floor. It was a large meditation hall with mattresses kept on the floor for many people to sit together. It had walls of glass, through which I could see the mountains and the lake.

"Guruji, I felt the positive energy around me when I stepped here for the first time. Now, after meeting you, I have no doubt that my life is going to change forever. I am blessed to be in your company," I said with folded hands as I sat in front of him.

"You are living in a paradise, I must say, Guruji."

"When I came here thirty years ago, I was transfixed to see the beauty of this place. I had decided to develop this place into something approachable so that people can come here and experience inner peace."

"Guruji, I had lost this peace of mind ever since I saw the person whom I loved with all my heart, moving away from my life. I cannot say how dejected, lonely and worthless I have been feeling over the last few months. Now, I am in your care. I came here to seek advice. Now, all that I need are your blessings and company and I will be able to discover a path to true happiness on my own. It has just been a few moments, but I can already feel the miracle of your company." I finished my words quickly before my voice got choked with emotions.

I folded my hands in reverence.

"God has given this experience to you for a reason. When you open your eyes after keeping them closed for a long time, the world outside looks brighter. In fact, it appears so bright that you have to cover your eyes for a few seconds. Similarly, you have been blinded by love for a few months in the past. Now, as you gradually open your eyes, you are going to see a brighter and clearer picture of life and the world. Ask any patient who has got his eyesight back after many years. They dance with joy on seeing this beautiful world. They can feel the magical difference after opening their eyes. You are also going to get the same enlightening realisation now. Be ready to experience immense happiness and rejuvenation." The monk was speaking in a flow in a calm and slow voice.

I kept listening to him, keeping my eyes closed. I must have been listening to him for more than fifteen minutes. Then, I opened my eyes.

The monk was talking to me, but was looking at the distant horizon, as if what he was saying was written in the sky.

His eyes were transfixed. In a very surreal voice, he said, "A rejection in love gives you an intense feeling. The power of the whirlwind of emotions is unparalleled. When someone goes through a breakup, the intensity of these sentiments is so high that if you channelize this energy in the right direction, you can help transform this world in a magical way. Is it easy to turn the direction of this energy in the right direction? Not really. But is it feasible?"

He paused for a moment and then started staring at me. His gaze was strong and his expressions unexplainable. I could not withstand the flame of his looks and blurted out as if to break the unending stream of uneasy silence.

"I agree with you Guruji. The feelings which are experienced after a breakup are really strong. But, can one really use them in a positive way? I would be surprised if this could be feasible."

After looking at my perplexed gaze, he said further, "Think of a dam which is holding a huge reservoir of water. It's an old dam which has led to a rise in the level of water and the formation of a huge lake which looks almost like an ocean. This ashram has been built beside such an artificial lake created due to the backwaters of a dam. There were many sluice valves designed to control and regulate the flow of water stored in the dam. During rainy seasons, the dam was filled up completely and there was a risk of the ashram getting flooded with water. I cannot forget the scary sight during the rainy season.

"Many people deputed at the site of the dam used to ask us to vacate the ashram. But we never did so. We had been living and meditating here for many years and we just could not imagine leaving the divine site. Finally, the government allowed us and designed the dam accordingly so as to keep this area safe. I know the immense power of water which is channelized by the erection of this dam.

"Now, you might be wondering why I am telling you the story. So let me explain. Many people don't know this, but I also had gone through severe depression due to heartbreak in my teenage years. In fact, it happened a few times in my early life. I found that every time I suffered heartbreak, I turned extremely creative. I painted some brilliant masterpieces. Once, I made a huge piece of art using only toothpicks. It was a portrait of lord Ganesha. During those days, I noted one thing. Had I not fallen in love and gone through some painful experiences, I would never have created some of the most amazing pieces of art. The emotional storm which I had contained within me after the 'loss' was now leading me to some of the unseen paths of creativity in an organic manner.

"When I came to the Himalayas, I realised the connection between the power of emotions which reside within us and the water that was held by the dam. Huge backwaters have limitless force hidden within it. However, this force needs a constructive system to channelise so that it can run hydraulic turbines, which in turn generate power. This power is transmitted to nearby villages and cities to provide electricity and comfort in the lives of people. The energy latent in water could have been unknown to the world had people not made a *system* to use its power for a constructive reason. In the absence of a system, the water had the ability to destroy everything that came in its way.

"Then I started thinking of the *creative power of a breakup* and the ways to utilise this to transform someone's life forever. I researched this subject extensively to discover some common patterns. Taj Mahal would have never been built if it were not for a deep sense of loss. Many authors, sportspersons, actors, entrepreneurs and artists had used their sorrows to make history. All they required was discipline and a positive mindset. The more I studied, the more confident I grew about the common patterns of transformation. Would you like to hear of these patterns which I discovered?" he took a pause and reached towards a glass of water.

"Yes, for sure!" I chuckled in excitement.

"Good, so let me share with you a few common trends. I noted the following ways to come out of the state of inaction and move ahead with full vigour and enthusiasm. It was important to get rid of all the gifts and mementos which made me think of her. I donated these gifts which she had once given to me to a nearby orphanage. It made me feel at peace. Now my mind had started thinking of other things which also mattered in my life and career. From staying focussed towards the happiness of only one person, I was slowly becoming aware of a whole new world of human connections, valuable friendships and possibilities. My worldview broadened as I had started becoming a part of a larger world," the monk said.

I was listening to him with utmost attention. He continued.

"We get all the cues of life mostly through our ability to see, hear, touch, taste and smell. These are our sensory organs. Till you keep such gifts at your place, you see the gifts and it reminds you of your past days of glorious love. In your mind, you run those moment of excitement and pleasure again and again like a broken record. With each round of remembrance, your longing for the old days becomes stronger and you think of making that one more call to bring your lover back into your life. The other person has moved on but you are still stuck in the old days.

"But, what you don't realize is that every day, it's a new morning. It's a new day of possibilities. Every day trees grow a bit more and new leaves come on old branches. Every day, the world changes a bit. Every day, god wants you to do more, be more and create more to make your life happier, healthier and more successful. Every day, the problems of this world beckon you with the hope that you will help alleviate some of the challenges.

"You can do so much more in a day. But no! You are still staring at those lifeless and meaningless gifts which you had got from someone who in fact has ceased to exist in your life. Time has changed and you are still stuck in the past. Hence, just empty your room of those gifts. Make room for new things to come. Life is like a tree. It sheds old leaves and wears the new ones. You are still wearing the old leaves. It's time for you to make space for the new things. Welcome life in its new avatar, Rohan. It will turn beautiful."

The monk had now closed his eyes and was breathing slowly. He was calm and relaxed. His posture was straight and upright. He was in a state of trance.

I realised all the mistakes which I had committed in all these months by still staying stuck to the old world around me. I had forgotten to give a compliment to my near and dear ones who had done something good. I had forgotten to say 'thank you' to my father who was worried about my well-being and was around me whenever he could. I had turned selfish. I was lost in my own pain so much so that the sorrows of others had ceased to matter to me.

I closed my eyes and sat straight, just like the monk. It was a state of calmness and peace within me. I stopped thinking of the monk or anyone around me. I heard the sound of swaying of leaves. I heard the babbling sound of flowing water nearby. I heard the sound of chirping of birds. I started noticing the sounds, which did not exist for me. I was surprised.

*Why did I not hear these sounds earlier? I had stopped listening to the loud sounds of pain and cries of people around me. I had stopped noticing the pain of my family. What to talk of the sound of subtlety? What a fool I was! Life was happening around me in its full glory and colours; and here I was – focussing all my attention and energy on just one thing – memories of the person who had left my world so long ago!*

"You can open your eyes anytime you wish," I heard the monk saying softly.

I opened my eyes with a deep sense of calmness and peace.

"That is the beauty of meditation. I know you have started enjoying it now. However, this is just the beginning. There are so many beautiful things of the world waiting for you. Now you probably get a hint of what I was indicating towards."

I nodded in affirmation, though I did not say anything.

"Now comes the second thing you are going to do. Please delete her number from your phone. You make sure that you have deleted her number from all your phones or devices." The monk was smiling.

I took a breath to process his words. Then, I followed his instructions.

"Tell me something about your hobbies and things you used to love doing once upon a time," the monk spoke.

I was wondering what he meant. I had to actually think for a while to remember the things I always loved doing.

"I used to love reading books. I used to love going on long drives. I used to love driving to woods and mountains.... I also used to love playing piano," I blurted.

"Used to... means what? Do you not practise these now?" the monk asked.

"I have been just too busy. I mean, I did not find time to pursue hobbies," I said.

"Find time now," the monk said. "You must find some time now to pursue your hobbies. Develop a new passion. I want you to get your mind occupied with a new way of engagement. I want your mind space to be filled with a new exciting routine or habit you are going to build," he said.

"But how is that going to help me? I could not get you. Would you mind elaborating it a bit?" I asked.

"Look, when you undertake a new hobby or start pursuing a new passion, it does many things to you. First, you start speaking a new set of words. You might have noticed that each field of life – be it sports, reading, teaching, driving, aeronautics or any profession – has a certain vocabulary. A new hobby will make you use these specific words, which directly affect your thoughts and broaden your mind. This will take your mind away from the usual thoughts of losing the love of your life.

"Secondly, a new hobby will make you find new friends. You will find new people who also pursue that particular hobby. This will change your company. You become the average of few people whose company you keep most of the time every day. As you start building new networks, you will start thinking of new things, saying new words and working on new projects. That is the power of your company. It changes almost everything about you.

"The third change is that you will start finding new pathways of happiness, joy and engagement and that gives a new meaning and path to your life. And the fourth thing is that your limitless energy that was pent up within you after the heartbreak will find a new channel. The same energy, which could have been released in negative ways of anger, frustration and envy, is getting channelized in a positive direction as you pursue your hobby more often.

"The fifth change that you feel is that you begin to learn something new in your life. The process of learning something new has a magical effect on your psychology. You begin to feel more enriched and fulfilled. You begin to feel more empowered. You begin to get a new meaning in your life. Over the last few months, you had stopped learning something new. You had stopped growing. You had turned into stale water, which starts stinking. Learning something new makes you feel stronger and more enriched.

"The sixth benefit is that you become an action taker. From being in a state of inaction, you become someone who has started doing something. From being a person who was only lost in his thoughts, you become someone who has started coming to a state of motion. All of a sudden, from being a puddle of dirty stale water, you become a stream of flowing water as you have started moving now. This is how pursuing a new hobby helps you get rid of your sadness of losing someone you loved. This is how pursuing a hobby makes you tide over your heartbreak."

The monk stopped after a long monologue. He had closed his eyes. His posture had become straight and erect. He was in a state of meditation. I also closed my eyes and started thinking of what the monk had just told me. I was sitting there with my eyes closed for some time till the monk's words broke the silence prevailing there.

"So, which hobby you are going to pursue now?" asked the monk.

"I will go for a destination walk everyday now. I will also begin to play piano once again..." I said, feeling a positive energy flowing within me.

I lived in the ashram for a few days and performed meditation with other members every day. I used to take long strolls along the lake. I also listened to the wise thoughts of the monk every day in the morning and evening. I used to eat healthy and spent some good time in the company of nature.

I could see the change now, and I knew the monk was right. I was becoming a new person now. Perhaps, Swami Rohananand or something like that!

♋

It all continued for a week before I got my next text message from Jayesh.

After exchanging some pleasantries, he wrote, "Dude. You are at a place I came to many years ago. I am sure you had a great experience. Now, it's time for you to travel to another place which will be another great experience and will be impossible to forget. You will get the car booking confirmation and accommodation details in following messages. Enjoy."

"Yogic Village." I saw my next destination address. It was in lower Himalayas near the foothills of the divine mountains near Haridwar. My journey down to the plains had started, but not before I took a halt in Yogic Village which was the beginning of the plains as I descended from the Himalayas.

I was ready and excited for my third destination while playing the game of life.

# 7

# *The Yogic Village*

As the car started moving out of the ashram, I could see that we were now going downhill along the valley. It raised a lot of dust along the road where construction work was going on at the dam site. The road ahead became a little hazy. Bubbles of dust reminded me of my life which did not have any clarity. I had lost a clear sense of direction in my life ahead. I strongly needed a goal in my life to dispel the haze which had surrounded my life.

As the road became better and the haze of dust was replaced with clean air, I wondered.

*Will I get back clarity and focus in my life?*

The journey of three hours was full of reflections on how I had lost track of things happening around me. All that I was thinking of was the girl who had enveloped my thoughts in every sense. The health of my mother, financial burden on my father, ills of the society I was living in – everything else had ceased to matter for me.

Beside the road, I saw many small and big temples and the priests who were walking around the temples. I saw some nomadic priests who seemed to have dedicated their life to the worship of gods and goddesses. They all looked completely focussed on one aspect – spirituality. The clothes they wore, the place where they lived and the expression which they carried on their face indicated that they had completely surrendered to their divine master.

*Was I any different from them? I also had completely surrendered my whole existence to the happiness of the girl I was in love with.* The central emotion between the priests and me was to surrender oneself. We had surrendered to different entities.

The priests and *sadhus* did all that they could to attain blessings of the divine being. I did everything that I could do to attain the love of the person I wanted to always be with. Did we get to our respective destinations? Did the sadhus get the blessings of the gods and goddesses?

According to *Bhagwad Gita*, we have the right over our actions and not on the fruit of the actions. Looks like I had missed an important point in the last few years of my life. I got confused into thinking that I also had the right over the fruit of my actions.

*But did I not get any fruit at all?*

Today, I realised that I had got many things as a result of the failed love. Let me count the blessings hidden in the heartbreak: I wanted to make a change in my life and that is the reason I had decided to come to the Yogic Village. I had some inkling that the place was about to change the course of my life.

Had it not been for the heartbreak, I would never have decided to spare some time and come to this place for my emotional and spiritual healing. I had become stronger by facing and surviving through one of the strongest emotional jolts I had come across.

I was now better aware of the feeling of love. Had I not gone through the experience, I would never have known the true feeling of being lovelorn. I would never have understood the emotion of Mirabai being lost in the love for lord Krishna.

I understood that love could be of different forms. Love for parents, love for friends and love for a girl – these are completely different feelings despite being the forms of the same 'love'. It is like any other thing in this world, which looks the same from a distance but as you go closer, you see different shades of the same thing.

Slowly, I was beginning to understand that what I thought to be love was mere physical attraction. It was not love. I understood that the world is a matter of perception. Einstein had propounded the theory of relativity. I found it to be true in my life. Now, I was on the path of self-discovery. I was having new realisations and was somewhere hopeful of getting a better meaning of life, success and happiness.

I reached Yogic Village in a few hours. As I got down from the cab, I saw roads with colourful flowers on both sides. The roads went deep inside the Yogic Village campus. There must have been thousands of flowers as the two roads, which I saw inside the village, were surrounded by shrubs of flowers till my eyes could see. Both the roads were straight paths and seemed to go for at least a kilometre. I saw flowers all along the roads. One road was straight in front of me and the other cut to my left.

Our car had just moved out through the dry river bed. Well, it seemed to be a rivulet, which must be coming down from lower Himalayas. Later, I was told that the Yogic Village was located at the confluence of two rivulets, which came to life in rainy season. In other seasons, the rivulets ran dry.

As I entered the gate of the yoga centre, the world changed almost in a magical way. I saw a world of flowers, neatly manicured gardens, a lake with a beautiful island and cottages for meditation, therapies and living. It was green and serene all along.

"Sir, you have to make an entry in the register," I was interrupted by one of the security men.

"Oh yes, sorry, I was lost in the beauty of flowers. You are working at such a lovely place. You guys are lucky," I said.

"Sir, you will also realise how dark the place looks in the night. We hear the sound of wild animals every night. Inside the gate, it's beautiful. Outside, it is dark and dangerous. Anyway, you are safe here as electric fencing all along surrounds the place. Stay within the premises and you will enjoy," he said with a smile.

"Thank you for cautioning me," I smiled back and leaned on the registration desk to enter my details.

I had to leave the cab there. A golf cart came and my luggage was shifted from the cab to the cart. I sat on it and without making a noise; the cart began to move on the road on the left side. I was enjoying these silent vehicles. I was also thinking about what the security guard said to me.

This world has two sides to it. It has beautiful flowers and dangerous forests, all within it. We have people who support us and those who try to demean us. This is the law of the universe. There are small islands of enlightened spaces amidst oceans of darkness and doubts. Goodness is always in short supply. You don't need to make any efforts to grow weeds as they come up on their own. You need to put in hard work and make huge investment of time, money and efforts to grow flowers. I am sure that the person who had created the Yogic Village must have put in huge efforts to create this magnificent world. My cottage had come and the golf cart stopped after a few minutes of drive.

"Sir, there is your cottage – MK 22. You can get down here," the cart driver said with a smile. I saw that everything and everyone in the village was smiling. The flowers seemed to smile at me just like the driver did. I also smiled back and got down.

"Why is the cottage named as MK?" I asked.

"Sir, MK stands for '*Muniraj Kutiya*'. Here, we have four different types of cottages – *Tapaswi Kutiya, Muniraj Kutiya, Rishiraj Kutiya and Devarshi Kutiya.* These basically mean a sage's cottage. But as you know, even among sages, there was a hierarchy." The driver smiled and bade me goodbye.

I took my luggage to the cottage and opened the door. It was a spacious cottage with basic amenities of life. The cottage had a table and chair. It had a *jhula* inside, which seemed to be the main attraction of the room. It had an attached bathroom and a bedroom. What looked like a plain cottage from outside was actually a place with amazing amenities.

I dropped my luggage in the bedroom and slumped on the jhula. It started swaying as I sat on it. I just lied down on it and pushed the ground a bit to make it sway longer. The complete silence was only broken by the sound of the rocking of the swing. It was a beautiful swing with wooden carvings. There was some light coming from the windows and door. The door was left open. There was no one around the cottage now. It was almost 9 a.m. now. The daily routine in the 'village' began early in the morning at 4 a.m. when people had to wake up. After doing meditation and yoga, they had a light breakfast before going for their treatments. This was probably the largest centre for naturopathy treatment in the country.

Gradually, I understood that we all should have been practising these rituals on our own. They taught us something as basic as valuing the treasure of ancient Indian rituals and methods of living healthy, happy and rejuvenated. They taught us the ancient magical rituals, which we have forgotten by now. Had we remembered even few of these secrets, we would never have fallen prey to despondent times. We would have understood the true meaning of life.

To enhance my knowledge further, I had researched about their guiding philosophies and found the following five key areas that they focus on:

First, they teach people how to develop a positive mindset. They teach us the laws of the universe. This universe is a magical world, they say. Though I am yet to realise which magic they are talking about! For me, it was magical till the girl I loved was in my life. Once she left, the magic also vanished. But here they teach you that the magic lies within you. You do not have to depend on others to seek your inner light.

Second, they also teach us the mindset of a learner. You have to learn constantly. The founder of this place, who is an internationally-acclaimed personality by now, enjoys a miraculous followership. But he still takes out at least one hour every day to learn something new from books, people or nature.

Third, they talk about the power of yoga. This is one ancient ritual which connects body and mind to the source of their creation. They say that it's possible to cure almost any disease, be it physical or mental, with this practice. The condition is that you have to practise yoga every day for at least some time.

Fourth, they talk about the power of Naturopathy. This is the source of attaining good health. Naturopathy, as they say, is all about 'returning to nature'. They believe in nature's power of healing.

Fifth, they teach you the power of Ayurveda. This includes consumption of herbs and spices, which cure specific diseases. Many yogis and saints spent all their lifetime while living in high Himalayas and forests in different parts of the country. In their lifespan, they learnt the power of many herbs and wrote about the healing and curative power of these in many ancient epics.

Sixth, they introduce people to the so-far-hidden magic of *yajna* or *havan*. I have read that in a corner of this beautiful premise, they have kept a *yajna kund* where anyone can go and offer *havan* and *aahuti* throughout the day. Yajna purifies the environment and uplifts the spirit of people to a higher level.

I was thinking about all that I had read and learnt about the place when I heard a gentle knock on the door.

"*Om,* sir. I have brought some healing water for you."

My train of thoughts was interrupted. I got up from the swing and opened the door. A man in white dress smiled and gave me a jug of warm water.

"Sir, here is some lukewarm aloe vera water for you", he said smilingly.

He moved on to the next cottage and I, after keeping the jug safely on the table, decided to venture out to have a look at the beautiful garden outside the room. It was a serene view.

There were cottages in C-shape which opened to the road leading to the office, canteen, meditation centre and therapy zones. It was a beautiful grassy land with a fountain in the centre. It appeared as if the fountain had not been operated for long.

Just across the road, I saw a beautiful lake with an island in the centre. There were boats of different colours anchored beside the lake. A hanging metal and wooden bridge led one to the island. It was an arched bridge, which one normally got to see in Japanese gardens. The island had a place covered by a little canopy. Looked like, it was meant for people to meditate in silence while listening to the swaying of the bridge and babbling of water.

The water in the lake was still and calm, but the pumped water falling from the rocks in a corner to keep the water refreshed and recycled, made a faint burbling sound which was audible even from this side of the road where I was standing now.

I walked towards the road and saw a few people riding on a noiseless battery-operated golf cart. I was wondering why people did not walk on these roads surrounded by flowers and plants. Had they done some mindful walking; they would have enjoyed nature better. They would have appreciated the beauty of flowers of various colours.

Most of the people in this world are just rushing through life without appreciating the beauty which is present all around them. They are not able to appreciate the magic of nature. I have friends who are working in high-end companies and know how their managers are so busy trying to live up to the expectations of their clients that they forget to appreciate the good work done by their team members.

It was late in the afternoon and it was time for me to take a bath, change my clothes and go to the main office as I had an appointment with the main doctor who was known for his brilliance in Naturopathy. I wanted to ask him a few questions on how to stay positive, happy and healthy, even after suffering from some of the most depressing moments in my life over the last few months.

♋

I was waiting in front of the doctor's cabin. I saw people with all kinds of health problems waiting in the queue ahead of me. They were sad and depressed. But I also noticed one thing. As they came out of the cabin after consulting the doctors, they seemed to carry an expression of relief on their face. I could see a change in their energy levels.

Meanwhile, I got a call on my phone from Jayesh

"Hey, how are you doing? How is your sojourn in the Himalayas?"

"You have planned it; it has to be nice," I said with a smile.

"Just nice? I thought you would say it's incredible and outstanding. Learn to enjoy man!" Jayesh seemed to be happy to hear the excitement in my voice.

"I think you have called me a little too early. Had you called me after a few days of my stay at this nice place, my answer would have been different, I guess. I am just in front of the cabin of the doctor and the healer. I can see that the people who come out after their meeting, have a shine on their face. Maybe, I would also feel better after the meeting," I said in a neutral tone.

"I am sure you would feel better. Cheers man!" he was exuberant and disconnected the call.

After a few minutes, the person who had gone to meet the doctor before me came out of the cabin. I entered the cabin after pushing aside the curtains at the door. The doctor was smiling at me. His face was shining. He had white shining hair and sported a French cut beard. I saw kindness in his eyes and a gleam on his cheeks. He did not appear to be a man in his early seventies as I had been told. He looked much younger.

"Come on in, young man! Why do you look so serious, as if the burden of this entire world is resting on your shoulders?" Our conversation had started off on a light note.

I smiled awkwardly. I saw two empty chairs kept in front of a large table in front of his chair. His body language was oozing confidence and composure.

"I was having a look at your medical card. I was told that you are under depression? Could you tell me more about it?"

"Sir, I don't find anything around me interesting. Nothing makes me happy. I mean, I am feeling better now over the last few days after visiting a few good places. But prior to that, it was as if the whole world had lost its meaning and nothing seemed to cheer me up. I don't know if this is called depression," I murmured.

"You are thinking of something from the past or the future. That is a problem. First, you need to learn to live in the present moment. You need to see the beauty around you. Do you practice meditation and *pranayama*? If not, you have to sit in silence for a few minutes before doing anything when you wake up in the morning. By the way, at what time do you normally wake up in the morning?" he asked.

I was a bit surprised.

*What type of question was this!* I thought, he would give me some pills and medicines to cure my depression. But the conversation had started on a surprising note.

"I wake up late, after 7 a.m. on a normal day. I wake up early only on the days that I have to catch a flight or train. Or else, I just cannot wake up early."

"You are waking up late and are beginning your day with a very low energy level. If you want to hasten the speed of your recovery to joyful days, you need to wake up early and practice silence, meditation and pranayama. I am writing about some changes in your medical diary which you need to build in your food habits. Human body is magical. You eat anything like bread, fruits or vegetables, it will convert these into muscle, blood and bones. You are what you eat. I want you to make a change in your eating patterns, which will drive your depression out of your mind," the doctor said and smiled.

He continued further, "For your daily eating routine, eat a bowl of roasted flaxseed mixed with curd and some salt. It will taste good as well. Take 'ABC juice', which consists of the richest sources of vitamin A, vitamin B and vitamin C. You take carrots, beetroot and amla; cut these into small pieces and put these in a juicer-mixer. Do not forget to add some water before starting the juicer. The outcome will be a red-coloured juice, which will always keep your health growing, and your face shining like never before. You will not need any vitamin supplement ever.

"I would also like to tell you about a fruit which acts like a powerful anti-depressant. This is rich in colour, tastes sweet and uplifts the mood, keeping you positive. Can you make a guess?" he asked.

"Mangoes?" I tried answering.

"No, it is black grapes. This fruit is a well-known cure for many neural diseases like Parkinson's and Alzheimer's and is a proven cure for depression. There are many natural chemicals in this fruit which will help you. You have to make it a habit to eat a few black grapes every day. Banana is another fruit which would be very good for your health. Both these fruits are powerful anti-depressants.

"Also, I suggest that you take a drink before going to sleep. This will consist of hot milk, turmeric powder and few dried black grape resins. Add some black dried grape resins and turmeric powder to milk and boil the mix. Drink a glassful of this warm milk. A chemical called curcumin found in turmeric helps increase the level of serotonin in your brain, which makes you happy. Take sprouted grains every day.

"On a physical level, doing *asanas* is very important to enhance the secretion of serotonin in your brain. You can do various types of *asanas* like Bhujangasan, Padmasan, Surya Namaskara, Setu-bandhasan, Mandukasan, Naukasan, Gaumukhasan and Markatasan every morning. Even if you do some of these asanas for a few minutes every day, you will start experiencing the transformation in the way you are thinking and live your life.

"Take a bowl of salads which is made after boiling carrot, beetroot, broccoli and sweet corns. Add some olive oil, lemon juice and rock salt to it and it will taste great. Take some oatmeal at night."

Then he began to write the recipes and eating plan in my medical card, which was also known as the medical diary in Yogic Village. I stayed silent for a minute or so until he finished writing in my medical diary. I had been looking around the room. There was a huge painting of Goswami Tulsidas on the wall. It depicted Goswami Tulsidas writing *Ramcharitmanas* on the steps on the bank of river Sarayu in Ayodhya. There was a halo behind the head of Tulsidas. I noticed a smile on his face.

"You like this painting?" he intercepted my thoughts and without waiting for my response, he said further, "When a person undergoes depression, their brain suffers from acute lack of dopamine and serotonin hormones. These are happiness hormones. Due to lack of these hormones, your depression becomes even more serious. The more you think negatively, lesser is the secretion of hormones. Lesser is the secretion, more acute your depression becomes. You can see, it's a loop of negativity which takes a downward turn in the journey of life." He took a pause.

I turned my gaze towards the painting of Swami Tulsidas on the wall and said, "Yes. I am intrigued by the stories written by him. How could he write an epic?"

"He wrote because, like you, he also underwent heartbreak," he was smiling again. It was a smile mixed with kindness.

"Heartbreak? He was a saint. How could he undergo heartbreak?" I asked.

"He had a fallout with his wife when she got angry with him for his obsessive behaviour towards her. She taunted him to show the same affection towards lord Rama in which case his life would be transformed like never before," the doctor said.

"Oh I see. I never thought that the author of *Ramcharitmanas* also had gone through what I have gone through recently. This is one common thread between me and Swami Tulsidas," I said.

"Heartbreaks are a way of life. You suffer a breakup at every turn of this journey called life. But the magical thing is – every breakup has a seed of major transformation hidden within it. We have the first 'breakup' when we are separated from the umbilical chord of our mother. The same umbilical cord, which has been feeding the baby for its first nine months of growth, is severed from the baby's body. That is the first step of transformation when the baby comes out of the protection of the mother's womb into this world. For the first time, the baby has to put its organs to test. The heart expands with the first breath that the baby takes. The lungs begin to suck air with each breath. They start pumping oxygen to the heart, which in turn, sends the oxygen to different parts of the body by mixing it with the blood. The body starts moving like a well-synchronised machine. The baby can open its eyelids and see the parents. It can hear the sound of the world. It can move its fingers and touch its mother. This is the first transformation in the life of a baby, emanating from a 'breakup'.

"The journey of life has just taken off and the baby begins to grow into a child. It rolls on the bed and floor of home. It cannot get up on its own. Afterwards one day, the baby 'breaks up' the connection with the floor and takes the first step. It moves up and falls with a thud. It does not accept defeat and moves up once again. After failing to get up and falling each time, it finally learns how to stand on its feet and walk. The baby becomes a child after suffering from the second breakup.

"Then, the child has to break the comfort of the home and go to a pre-nursery school. The parents become emotional to even think of the child going to school for the first time. The child first cries at the fear of breaking up from the comfort zone of home. But these 'tears of fear' are replaced with the fun of finding new friends in the pre-nursery school and learning new traits of life. The child grows up and then suffers another breakup while moving out of their home to build their life.

"As we grow up, the world around us will force us to harbour the same dream. We are ridiculed and laughed at by the society for wanting to take a different path. We, despite knowing that our biggest success stories are hidden behind tall mountains of risks, are not able to climb that mountain. We decide to live all our life in the shadow of the mountain in the safety of the foothills. We see just a few people climbing the mountain and discovering a new world. You should not take this breakup from the girl you loved so seriously. You should be more concerned about your 'breakup from your dreams'. This one breakup you should never allow...." He stopped for a while and took a glass of water.

I stood stunned there. I never had any realisation like this.

"I thought you are just a naturopathy doctor. But I think you are a mentor and motivator as well. I am feeling so refreshed after spending some time with you. I am shaken by your words. I am just realising how unfaithful I have been towards my life. Whatever I am today is the result of various breakups I had. Then, how can this one breakup make me suffer and dampen my spirits? This also must be meant to make me stronger and transform my life forever. Please suggest how to deepen my realisation so that I can take actions and pursue a new direction in my life."

"Rohan, you need to write your diary every day. In the diary, write down at least one new opportunity which is waiting for you every day. This new opportunity can be in the form of a new meeting with a customer, a coffee with an old friend with whom you had lost touch over last the few years or a new project in the office.

"This can be in the form of a new book, which you are going to begin reading today. This also can be in the form of a new mentor or navigator you are going to meet, just like you met me. Opportunities are in abundance and are spread all around you at every place. You just need to do your *karma yoga* and keep moving. Like a Chinese bamboo tree, nothing may happen and not even a sapling will be visible for five years if you keep watering the seed, which you had sown in the soil.

"In an almost mystical way, the seed will not break through the ground for the first five years. But if you keep watering the seed, take god care of it and allow it a fertile soil and sunshine, a small sapling appears after five years and then it reaches up to a height of ninety feet in just five weeks. Now the question is – did the seed grow to ninety feet in only five weeks or five years? It is of course five years plus five weeks because had you stopped watering the seed during the first five years, the seed would never have sprouted and the sapling would never have come out. You need to put in consistent hard work and maintain your courage.

"In summary – eat well, stay positive, stay inspired and keep moving in the direction of your dreams and goals. And yes, like all other breakups, this heartbreak will also lead you to a better, bigger and more beautiful world. Trust me." He said and smiled.

I got up, folded my hands to pay my respect to him, and turned back to leave the cabin. My voice was choked with emotions to think of the harm I had been causing myself.

Unlike other people, I was leaving his cabin with a trace of tears. These were the tears of joys. Now I knew why everyone leaving his cabin was in a state of enchantment!

The sunny day seemed more beautiful and grass on the lawn greener. It is true – our inner state of mind determines our outer happiness. I looked up at the sky and moved towards my cottage.

I stayed in the village for a week. My time there was spent doing yogasanas and pranayams. I used to take a walk in the lap of nature in the morning and evening hours. I took various ayurvedic treatments, including *shirodhara*, mud bath, steam bath, *ayurvedic* body massage and head massage. It was an amazing feeling!

After a week, in the evening, I got the next text message. I was surprised to see the discipline with which Jayesh was conducting the 'game of life'.

*But why was he doing all this for me? He could easily have sent the money to me or to my father after knowing about my disenchantment. Why was he doing all of this, I mean making a travel plan must have required a lot of time and effort.*

I knew I was going to ask him this question the day we met next. I opened the message with great curiosity.

*Hey dude.*

*Hope all is going awesome at your end.*

*Here is your next surprise destination. You have to leave the lap of Himalayas and enter the sand dunes of Rajasthan. Tomorrow, you will catch a flight from Dehradun to Jaipur. A car will be waiting for you outside Sanganer airport. It will take you via one of the finest and most beautiful highways to Ajmer. From there, it will take you across the barren hills to Pushkar. Well, it's not exactly Pushkar. It's a little out of Pushkar town. You will feel overjoyed to find yourself surrounded by tents, hills and of course, sand dunes.*

*Welcome to the land of brave-hearts who gave everything they had to protect their motherland. Welcome to the state of Rajasthan now. Below this message, you will find your air tickets and the name and number of the driver who will meet you in the pink city outside the airport. Bon voyage!*

*Love*
*Jayesh*

The following day, I started early in the morning. For some strange and unknown reasons, I had a feeling that my trip to Rajasthan was going to be the most exotic and memorable experience for me. I was wondering as the car meandered its way through the road on the outskirts of the city, moving towards the highway, which was to take me to Ajmer. It was my first trip to Jaipur, but there was something about the city, which I instantly fell in love with.

Well, 'love' is not a word I wanted to use anymore, but that is exactly what it appeared to be. I had started loving its barren look, colourful clothing, relaxed ambience, handicrafts spread beside the road at many places in the city and carts driven by camels.

*Will the sand dunes bring one more life-changing turn in my life?*

# 8

## Sand Dunes of Pushkar

When I came out of the Jaipur airport, the first thing that caught my attention was the display of handicrafts and hoardings of colourful people and dancers of the desert city. The airport did not have the look and feel of a busy business city like Pune or Bengaluru. It had the leisurely charm of a city known for its rich heritage, old and new buildings made of pink stones, tasty and spicy delicacies, people in colourful attire, endlessly large forts maintained in their old world charm, shops which sold a wide range of articles, including modern mobile phones and kites and some of the most luxurious forts and palaces.

I saw a unique sight while moving through the outskirts of the city. I saw many nomadic groups having settled in the open and barren lands at many road junctions. This reminded me of a chapter which I had read in my school books many years ago.

The major part of the state of Rajasthan is a beautiful desert. Hundreds of years ago, a large population of the state understood that the place will not have food for them, green pasture for their pet animals and water for their survival if they lived at one place all their life. This realisation gave rise to a new tribe in Rajasthan, known as nomads.

The population decided to keep visiting different places in the state throughout their life. They temporarily settled at a place where they got food and water. They moved to another place after the supplies were finished. They called the world as their own. They did not have any address or a permanent house. I used to find this phenomenon strange.

I remember, when I left my hometown for the first time to go out to a large city to pursue higher studies, I was in tears. I suffered from home sickness for long, till I somehow accepted the reality and started settling down in the new phase of my life. I still kept calling my parents from time to time every week to 'feel their proximity'. I was in my comfort zone.

*How could the nomads of this desert state get over their homesickness? How could they decide to keep moving to a new place every few months, till they lived? How could they think of making their new temporary hut or tent every few weeks and fought over the ever-changing weather? How could they become so comfortable with the idea of breaking out of their comfort zone every few weeks, all their life?*

Now, I have started understanding this secret. Human mind is powerful. It is flexible and adaptable. All you need to do is to train it well and see the magic. Until I kept looking back to my days of childhood after moving to the new city for higher studies, I kept crying and feeling sad. But once I 'trained my mind' to accept the new reality and study better in the company of some of the most competent students in the larger city, my life changed forever.

So, all that the nomads did many hundred years ago was to accept the reality that staying at one place would be harmful for them. They changed their mindset to that of 'seeing new places all their life'. They accepted the whole world – or at least the whole state of Rajasthan – as their native place. They passed on this message to the future generations. In subsequent generations, children got these lessons since their childhood days.

"Sir, we are on the highway to Ajmer now. We just left Jaipur behind. We will reach Pushkar in a few hours. I will stop the car after a while where we can take lunch," the chauffeur said.

Watching the dry and barren landscape, tents of nomads built every few kilometres beside the road, people in colourful dresses and large turbans and Khejri trees had a therapeutic effect on me. I slept observing all these things around me.

♋

My eyes opened when the car stopped after reaching the remotely located camp nestled in the lap of sand dunes on the outskirts of Pushkar. This is where the life transformation coach lived. He was also known as the Miracle Man (MM).

He was known for bringing unbelievable changes in the mindset of people. He was known as a coach who influenced the way people perceived their life. Once their thought process changed, their life also changed completely. Jayesh must have sent me here for a reason. It was not difficult to find why!

My first meeting with MM was memorable. His words were as inspiring as his young and shining personality. He wore a sparkling white jacket, kurta and pyjama. In the first meeting with him, I thought he was my Krishna. I was like Arjuna in the battleground of Kurukshetra, bewildered and confused.

"Rohan, we welcome you to the sand dunes of Pushkar. This place is known as the Motivation Villa. This is the place I always wanted to create in my dreams. A place, which has the capacity to accommodate five hundred people at a time, came up last year. Now, my next goal is to expand its capacity to five thousand people. I want to convert the sand dunes, which you see till your eyes can reach around this place, to a tent city where I can invite those who are depressed and lost. So that when they go back, they go with a mission to change their life and the life of millions of people in this world. I want the world to remain inspired," the coach said.

I bared my heart to him as I had done in front of the monk. He listened attentively.

"Rohan, for attainment of success and happiness in life, you need to focus on three things. This is a general principle and I have practised this in my life as well as advised many of my mentees to practise the triad of these success sutras. I can see that you are suffering from the same lack of focus on what truly matters to you."

The coach was sitting firmly on the mattress kept on the floor. His gaze on my face was as intense as the rays of the shining sun in the middle of a hot summer day.

"I have come here to get rid of a negative mental state. I want to be happy and content, but I don't know how to attain this goal. In fact, I never knew, being happy will become such a tough task. That one girl ruined my life and I have been feeling so helpless. I have come to your shelter in this desert town to see the greener pastures of life once again. I need your help. I am ready to do all that you suggest. Please bless me and help me come out of the dark clouds of gloom.

"I was about to give up and take my life, but somehow god planned for me to come to you. And now I can see why He did so! I have been to some nice places in the last few weeks and I have started experiencing a change in my perspective towards life. After coming here, I think, I will not need any other mentor. I will follow your suggestions. I want to do something as big as you have done," I pleaded as I felt tears trickling down my cheeks.

"Don't cry. Falling in love was not your mistake. Falling out of love was a part of your destiny. If you did not commit a mistake, why should you cry? I know you are sad, but this state of depression is not going to help you in any way. You have already punished yourself for long. Stop now. While the person who left your company does not have anything to do with your life now, you are still feeling the pain and suffering. It's high time that you change the path of your life."

"I will try my best, sir. But please give me your blessings. Please guide me on how to be happy and successful again," I said.

"First step on the journey of transformation is to have a deep realisation of the mistakes you are committing. I told you about the three basic tenets of success. I am going to tell you about each of these one after another, and I would like you to reflect on your life and see for yourself if you are following any of these.

First principle of success is to surround yourself with the company of people who inspire you and do not make you feel belittled. You start feeling, thinking and acting like the people with whom you spend the maximum time. If you want to understand the secrets behind successful people, look at their company. If you want to know why people fail, again make a list of people whose company they keep.

"Look at your company! You are surrounded by people who make you feel deprived and sad. They keep on asking you about the reasons of your breakup. Some of them have gone through a breakup in their own life and have lost a lot of time. Your friends might be showing pity on your condition. They might be telling you stories of their own breakups and making you believe that it's okay to feel sad on your condition. I guess, your playlist would be filled with music albums of sad songs. You might be looking at her social media profile and thinking of the old beautiful days of your life when she was with you. She is happy with her life after moving on and you are still caught in her thoughts. Can you imagine what a mess you have made of your environment?

"Great people maintain the company of inspiring people and heartbroken people keep the company of the distressed and depressed lot. You need to change your company immediately. I will ensure that there is complete change in your environment." The coach took a pause and closed his eyes. He sat in silence for a minute.

"I am finding solutions to all my problems. I am getting clarity in my life. My life is full of happiness."

I was a bit surprised to hear the coach say these words calmly and slowly while his eyes remained closed.

I did not know how to react. MM opened his eyes momentarily and said calmly, "Repeat after me!"

I closed my eyes and started following what the coach said.

*I am finding peace in all my life experience.*

*I am getting happier with each passing day.*

*I am getting healthier day by day.*

*I am using my breakup to bounce back in life.*

*My breakup is making me a better person.*

*I am a champion and winner of life.*

*I am the master of my destiny.*

The coach went on saying and I kept repeating all that he said. After a while, he stopped and so did I.

He opened his eyes.

"Thank you sir," I said.

"Why thanking me so early?" he asked smilingly.

"For saying these things on behalf of me. You said things like turning one's moments of breakup into the seeds of greatness. I felt good simply by saying so. But sir, what is the advantage of saying this? Do I get happier by just saying or repeating something?"

"We just practised incantations, which is nothing but saying positive sentences. As you do this, your subconscious mind begins to pick these statements and starts believing in these. If we practise affirmations every day, the sentences will get deeper into our conscience and subconscious mind and it is a proven fact that once your subconscious mind absorbs a feeling, thought or emotion, it makes it your reality," the coach said these words while looking into my eyes. He smiled and kept a genuine expression of empathy on his face. I found a sense of reassurance in his words and looks.

He further added, "From today, as I said, your new version is being born. You are going to become version 2.0 of yourself. This will require some changes to be made in your life. The first of these changes will be to begin thinking of positive things in your life. No negative thoughts are allowed from today onwards. Say aloud with me.

And he gestured at me to sit straight and follow his words. I was crouching by now, but straightened my posture immediately. I felt a slight strain in my back, but it vanished soon as I repeated five times along with the coach.

"I always think of positive thoughts. Life is turning more joyful with every passing day."

The coach turned his gaze towards a huge painting on the wall on his right. I saw the painting and was enamoured with it.

What a beautiful picture it was! It showed the sun rising above the sea. The sun was red in colour and looked brilliant with the backdrop of a yellow, orange and crimson sky.

"I have got this painting to remind me of the power of the rising sun. There has not been a single day in my life when I did not see the rising sun. You cannot change your life unless you change your habits. I will help you build some super powerful habits, but waking up early in the morning is one habit which can single-handedly steer your life in the right direction. This is because I am going to make you practise five things every single morning. With these morning habits, your life is going to take a new turn. Welcome to a bright and beautiful new world," the coach said.

He, finally and for the first time since I was talking to him, had a wide smile on his face.

"This second principle of success is to change your habits. In addition, you are going to make the third change in your life. That is to set massive goals in your life. You do not even know that you are wasting your days and nights while thinking about the person who decided to move away from your life, only to leave you in a state of disarray and confusion," the coach said.

"I have heard of goals, though I never set goals for myself. But I have never heard of massive goals. What is the difference between a 'goal' and a 'massive goal'?" I asked.

"Before I say this, I would like you to tell your subconscious brain that the third principle of success is to set massive goals in life. You can do this by writing and repeating your goals every day, preferably in the morning for some time. Best changes in life do not take much time. They just need will power. You won't even take ten minutes in reading and saying these goals.

"But as I said, set massive goals which seem almost impossible even to you. Our brain needs excitement. Think big and win big in life. Now, we break for today. Take rest and we assemble in the meditation hall tomorrow morning at 5 a.m." The coach said and left the place.

♋

Next morning was even more enchanting for me. MM shared his thoughts on the power of intention.

"Dr Wayne Dyer spoke of the power of intention. He spoke about twelve phases of intentions. If you have a strong intention of being happier and successful, everything in this universe will come together to help you achieve your goal of happiness. But the question is – are you willing to come out of the stage of self-pity, self-hatred, self-deprecation, self-delusion and almost a suicidal state of mind? Are you willing to have the intention of creating a world of greatness around you?" MM asked.

"I did not get you. I mean, are you saying that I am the only person to be blamed for all the evils of my life now? Are you saying that the girl who broke my heart and did not look back even for a moment to see what I was going through, is not to be blamed at all? I did what any ordinary human being would do. I loved her with all my heart. Is that my fault?" I asked with a quiver in my voice.

"No surprises that you are grieving like an ordinary human being. You loved like an ordinary human being and failed in love like an ordinary human being. Now, for a change, and since you have come to me, can you decide to behave like extraordinary people? Stop being average. Stop being normal as no one who has changed the world has ever remained a normal human being. The world is transformed by those who make a difference and propose a new thought process for others to emulate. They are known as the thought leaders. The ones who behave like most of the people do, live and die a normal or average life. Rise above the ordinary. Be extraordinary," the coach paused for a while.

I was stunned. I was feeling a little humiliated as well. I was not happy on the use of the word 'ordinary' for me. And I think he sensed it as he added further.

"See, you have to stop living the life of an ordinary person. I realised it the hard way personally. While your case is that of a breakup; mine was a case of failure. I see a similarity between both the stories. In both experiences, your heart aches; you feel abandoned; you feel at loss; you are in state of delusion and you desperately yearn for some more shine from the world. The reality is, when you need the shine the most, it is least expected to come to you. Nothing comes to a desperate soul. Desperation is a negative emotion. You also must have experienced it yourself. Do you recall the times when you needed her to come back in your life desperately, only to see her moving away from you even farther? That is what desperation does to you. If you want to regain love in your life, you need to stop showing desperation," MM said, while looking sternly into my eyes. His gaze made me feel uncomfortable.

He continued, "When I faced the lowest phase in my life after failing in my goals while working in the corporate life, I did what any other ordinary person would do. I cribbed, complained, blamed and shirked from taking responsibility of my status. I did not look within, nor did I take any action to change my life. The same story continued for some time and I did not get any solace from this mindset.

"I soon realised that I needed to respond in a different way. I needed to take extraordinary actions and wage a battle to gain freedom from the worries of my life. Instead, what I did was what you are doing now. I felt helpless. I felt that it was normal to feel the pain and go in a downward loop of negativity. I felt as if the world around me had cheated on me. I thought I was unlucky. I went to astrologers, looking for the right direction in my life. I started wearing lucky stones on my finger. I did everything possible to ward off the evils happenings in my life. However, I did not do that one thing which I should have done and which I am going to recommend to you now to do over the next few days."

MM was in a state of meditation for a minute or so. I could see the smile on his face getting wider and his face becoming calmer. Then he opened his eyes.

I was feeling excited in anticipation of being told the solution to make my life happier. I was almost in a hurry to hear the words which could have given me the answer to all my problems.

MM seemed to understand my curiosity. He seemed to read my mind as he said, "You are again committing the same mistake. You are being desperate to get the answer. Remember, what did I tell you a while ago? Desperation is a negative feeling and energy. You have to relax and calm down. I cannot give you a solution while you are in a negative state. Remember, the mindset of the receiver is more important than that of a giver or transmitter. Your phone should be in a state of reception or else it will fail to catch the signals emitted by the transmission tower. I am the transmission tower and you are the receiver. But are you in a state of receiving the message perfectly?" MM was smiling. He seemed to be having fun at my plight. I was getting agitated a bit.

"Look, the first lesson which you must internalise now is that desperation only attracts rejection and leads to frustration. Never show your desperation for love, promotion, money, health or kindness. Just be grateful for all that you already have received from god and destiny. The Universe will give you more if you are in a state of gratitude and less if you act out of desperation. If you feel grateful for the love which you got from your ex-girlfriend, you will feel calmer and will be in a state of receiving more love with time. Only the source of love will change, but leave that task to the Universe.

"You do your duties. Stop being ordinary. Be extraordinary. Love, live, forgive, smile, feel calm, enjoy nature, enjoy little blessings of life and life will smile at you.

"Let's do a little exercise. Can you please write down eleven things you should feel blessed for? Right now? Please take a pen and paper and do this exercise in the next fifteen minutes." He indicated towards the table where the stationery was kept.

I was in a state of disbelief. *How could I have written eleven things I was blessed with and that also in fifteen minutes? I was in the pain of loss and the world looked dark and dull. Was there any blessing at all for me?*

But I did not have a choice. I got up and took the pen and paper. I started writing as MM went out of the room for some time. I got busy thinking and writing. Soon it became easy for me because I realised that I had done this exercise earlier after returning from the slum area in Mumbai.

Now I thought I must write the statements of gratitude every day. I will be in a state of gratitude only if I do this ritual everyday, without fail.

"Okay. Let's discuss now." MM had returned. "You can stop writing now. Tell me something about how you felt when you started writing?" he asked.

"This has been an intriguing feeling. When I started writing, it seemed like such a tough task. I had to struggle to write the first few lines. It was a real struggle. But soon, it started becoming easier. In fact, I have already written eleven points as suggested by you and now I feel, I can write ten more. Honestly, I can write a hundred more points is what I feel now. But why did I not realise this earlier? I am wondering why I found it so difficult initially, despite the fact that I have done this exercise once in the past. I think I need to do this more often," I said.

"Daily. You should practice this daily. We are never in a state of gratitude. We count our pains and miseries more often than our blessings. This is what any ordinary person will do. And as I told you a while ago, you have been behaving like any other ordinary person all these months. Now, stop being average and ordinary. Count your blessings everyday and you will see a sense of peace and tranquillity showering on you like magic." MM took a pause before proceeding, "Can you read out a few points?" He asked with a question mark in his eyes.

"Yes, why not? Here are the points I have written," I said and started reading the points.

*I am blessed to have my father beside me. He wants to support me and make me happy once again.*

*I am happy that I can read and write as a lot of people are illiterate in the world.*

*I am blessed to have your company. After all, how many people can actually get in touch with you? They need to get guidance but do not have anyone as revered as you to provide them personal guidance.*

*I am blessed to be walking on my legs. There are millions who are bedridden even at this moment.*

*I am blessed to have a good educational qualification. There are a lot of people without the kind of degrees which I have with me.*

MM stopped me while feeling a sense of satisfaction.

"Good. That is beautiful. I can see that you have done a great job. You will realise that when you start writing or thinking of blessings, you struggle to think in the beginning. Then, you think of things which are more obvious. But as you resume this practice, you will realise that you are counting things which you took for granted till now. The problem is, we do not realise the meaning of things until we lose them. This is an ordinary thinking. Extraordinary thinking is to see the value of things while they are still there with you," MM said.

"Yes, I can appreciate this. People value health when it is gone. They value peace of mind when it is gone. They value money when they don't have much. They value love when it is gone. Today I decide and commit to you that I will value these while these are still there. I will count my blessings every day. I will count eleven blessings right in the morning. I will also write them so that I create my own journal of blessings..."

"Great. Now we take a break. Let us meet again in the evening and we will have another life-transforming talk. We will go through the twelve principles propounded by

Dr Wayne Dyer," MM said and smiled before getting up and leaving the hall.

I heard the sound of his footsteps for long as I sat there in silence with my eyes closed. I could realise that the things had started changing gradually within me. I opened my eyes and looked around. The world outside me had also started changing. I smiled and got up after thanking the coach in my heart and mind.

♋

I had a leisurely walk in the health resort in the day time. I was mesmerised to see peacocks strolling and running around on green lawns. There was a team of gardeners carefully watering flowers and the entire lawn area. There were beautiful benches full of carvings placed every fifty metres or so along the walkway. The resort had a jogging track all around it. Flowers, peacocks, lawns and water fountain; this place truly was a true reflection of the 'massive goal' which MM must have set for him.

I could not wait to meet MM in the evening. And my anticipation showed, I had once again begun falling in love; this time it was my love for life and positivity.

When I met MM in the evening, he highlighted the importance of being kind to oneself as well as others.

He said, "Be in a state of kindness. It has been found that those who give kindness, receive kindness. Giving or receiving kindness brings a sense of calmness and joy because of the secretion of serotonin. Create a sense of purpose in life and be kind to others. There are three ways to show kindness to others. It can be done by dedicating your time, efforts and money to be kind to others, especially those who need it. Now continuing our discussion on the power of intention, let me share the twelve points of 'the Dyer Dozen' and their relevance and meaning in your life. Have you heard of this term earlier?"

"No, I have not. But I would like to learn more about the Dyer Dozen. It sounds very interesting," I said with a visible sense of excitement.

MM started with his message for the evening. "Want more for others than you want for yourself was the first point said by Dr Wayne Dyer. Think of it. When was the last time you thought of others rather than thinking of your own self? I think, you will be surprised to note that all these months after you went through the breakup, you have been thinking only about your pain and loss. You need to rise above your personal loss and dedicate at least some time and energy for others and not for you."

I think he wanted me to '*feel* his words and think about these' later on.

He further added, "Think from the end, said Dr Dyer in his second principle. Always imagine the ideal life which you want to live. Think of the happiness which you want to have. You need to make a significant shift in your mind. From having the mindset of someone who is only crying at the loss of someone who gave you love, pleasure and pain, you need to completely transform yourself to become a person who is thinking about the life which you want to have."

"Dr Wayne Dyer's third law is to become an appreciator of life. What does that mean? It simply means that you have to grow in your life in all aspects. You have to grow in your happiness, your health and your career. Are you appreciating your life or deprecating it?" asked the coach.

I was silent. I was deeply lost in my thoughts. I was, for the first time, realising how badly I had lost my precious months while completely neglecting my own priorities.

"The fourth law of the power of intention is to stay in rapport with the source of life. This means, maintain your connect with the almighty who has given you this precious life. The best way to do this is to meditate regularly. When you sit in silence and meditate, you feel the connection with god who has created all of us. You have a deep realisation about your own body, thoughts and feelings. Tell me, when was the last time you became one with your creator? You have completely broken the rapport with the source of life." The coach was looking at me with silent eyes. I could feel the pain, which he was feeling at my life. And here was I, completely oblivious of the downward path my life had started taking.

"You also have to remember to keep away from any thoughts of resistance. Any thought which comes as resistance to your connection with the source which has made you, will fall under the category of resistance. Be kind to yourself, love yourself, give you a chance to forget your pains and be ready to welcome more love and abundance in your life. Only allow ideas, which will prepare you to seek more, be more and attain more of good things in life.

"Think of things which you want to see happening in life. Think of happiness which you want to attract in your life. Think of health and wellness, which you want to experience in your life. Think of people who you want to be surrounded by. Think of success which you want to see in your life.

"Understand the art of allowing. Allow the blessings of god to come to you. It is just like how you need to allow fresh breeze and oxygen to come to you if you want to feel refreshed. Unless you come out in the morning and go for a walk, you will not allow your body and mind to get the required amount of oxygen. Similarly, you need to introspect whether you are allowing happiness, blessings, peace, kindness and gratitude to come to you.

"Practise radical humility is the next point. This means, be humble to accept that it is human to lose people and resources. It is perfect to lose the person you loved. In fact, we all lose something or the other almost everyday. But we also gain lots of other things in our regular life. You gain a new sun everyday and lose the moon. You gain sunshine and lose moonlight. It all depends on how you look at life. If you look at morning as the 'loss of moon' and evening as the 'loss of sun', you will always lead a sad life. On the contrary, if you look at your morning as the 'gain of sun' and evening as the 'gain of moon', you will always live a happy life. The crucial point here is, do you have the mindset of looking at your loss as your gain and make it the pivot of your transformation?" MM was smiling now. I was getting intrigued at his thoughts.

"Be grateful for everything is the ninth life lesson Dr Dyer spoke of. Are you grateful for all that god has given you? God has presented you with health, wealth, family, a beautiful city, a home to live in and good education. But your mind has stopped seeing these gifts, just because one person has walked away from your life. The sun still shines. The moon still sparkles in the night. The days are still full of opportunities and the nights are still full of dreamy stars in the sky. Then what makes a person lose sight of these all of a sudden?

"Always remember that you cannot find solutions by criticizing someone. Do not criticize the person who is no more in your life. If you feel bitter about her, just forgive her. You can also do forgiveness meditation. Bless her for the loving moments she brought in your life, and move on. Life is all about experiences, which make your life fulfilling and enriching. You had some memorable experience out of this relationship. Just thank god for these moments and move on. Life is all about moving on and not about getting stagnant or stale. Always remember, if you condemn something or someone, you also attract negative energy from others. Have you not heard of the third law of motion by Newton? To every action, there is reaction.

"Last two points Dr Dyer emphasized while propounding Dyer Dozen include 'playing the match game' and practicing meditation.

"Meditation is the final point. You must do some form of meditation. You must spare some time in the morning hours to do meditation. Meditation is the best way to connect with the source of creation. You can realise that ever since you fell in love or lost the person you loved, you might never have meditated in your life. That means, you have lost your connection with the almighty. Meditation is also the best way for you to connect with your body, mind and soul. Unless you have the personal experience of it, you will never realise the power of self-discovery through an act of meditation.

"These are the Dyer Dozens and even if you build a few of these lessons, your life will get transformed forever," said MM before closing the evening session.

I was busy writing down each of the twelve points. I had decided to spend some time meditating over these points today before sleeping, as well as tomorrow after waking up. I had heard on the significance of meditation from the monk and the Naturopathy doctor as well. I was convinced that this is one practice I should do more often.

*It was probably the most enriching day in my life ever since I started playing the game of life.*

♋

I got up early the next day. It was still dark when I came out. The meditation centre was dimly lit when I entered. MM was sitting on a mattress in the centre of the hall. I went and sat in front of him.

"Today we will practise forgiveness meditation," I heard MM saying as I closed my eyes and tried focussing on his sayings.

"It is the perfect time for us to practise forgiveness meditation. It is said that if we hide and suppress certain negative feelings against someone else, it is somewhere hidden within our own body. If there is one person who suffers the most from these suppressed feelings, it is we, ourselves. Today, we need to learn how to forgive. I know you have been keeping certain feelings against someone. It's time to forgive her and move on with this beautiful life. Let us begin with affirmations," His voice resonated with the swaying breeze.

"I am happy. I am healthy. I can forgive easily. I can forget easily. If you look at the word forgive. It is made up of two words, 'for' and 'give'. Life is for giving. Similarly, forget is comprising two words, 'for' and 'get'. Life is for giving love and not only for getting love. I can forgive. I am peaceful. I am healthy. I am happy. The whole Universe is my friend. The entire universal power is with me now. Take a deep breath. Exhale through your mouth," MM went on saying slowly. I repeated the sentences in my mind while staying silent.

"Think of anyone whom you have caused pain. The pain could be of various types. Think of people who might have hurt you. Think of the person you loved and she also loved you for a while. It's time for you to forgive the person who has caused you disappointment. Imagine that she is standing in front of you. You are standing at an elevated platform. You have grown in your size and she is there along with others who have disappointed you. These people are from your office, neighbourhood, friend-circle or family. Along with these people, you also see her standing in front of you.

"Imagine that a beam of pink light is emanating from the sky and coming down to the earth. It comes down directly to you and gently touches the tip of your head. The beam of pink light starts entering your head and from there, it enters your neck, chest and the rest of your body. Your entire body is filled up with pink light. This light is full of the warmth of wellness and nurturing. This light heals your body and mind and then begins to travel towards other people. This pink light enters the body of others who are standing in front of you with folded hands. The pink light spreads throughout their body and heals them as well. They feel calmer, healthier and happier. They thank you for sending the healing light and energy towards them. They are telling you, 'I am sorry. Please forgive me. I am sorry, please forgive me.' They have the feeling of repentance in their eyes. They genuinely want you to forgive them. You also join your hands as a gesture of pleading forgiveness.

"You also say, 'I am also sorry. I beg for your forgiveness. I know I also have committed mistakes and caused you unhappiness. I know by now that you need two hands to clap. If you have disappointed me, I also must have disappointed you. I am sorry. Please forgive me.' They also are asking for forgiveness.

"As you and the people standing in front of you say sorry to each other, the pink light spreads faster and encircles you and the people in front of you. The pink light has engulfed you and the people from head to toe. You are feeling lighter. They are also feeling lighter. She is feeling lighter. You hear chirping of birds on the trees around you. Leaves on the tree are swaying with the breeze. You can feel the gentle touch of the breeze on your body. Sun is shining and spreading warmth all around. It's a beautiful blue sky. The pink light is vanishing inside your body and the body of other people standing in front of you.

"Now gradually, you see the people in front of you vanishing into thin air. They slowly vanish and leave a trace of pink light. Now you see only yourself standing in front of you. It's like a mirror image of you is standing facing you. You are forgiving yourself. You are smiling. Your reflection is also smiling. You say, 'I forgive me. I forgive me for whatever happened. I am sorry. God, please forgive me. I thank you god for forgiving me.'

"Now bring a smile on your face. Imagine that the whole world is back to normal. You are happy. Everyone around you is happy. All the animals around you are happy. The world has become the perfect place to live. You and others are smiling and feeling the inner happiness. Everything is perfect. The world is perfect. Your world is perfect.

"Your reflection vanishes and now you are standing in a state of bliss and joy. Now you can bring both your hands together and rub them. You can gently place your palms on your eyes. You can feel the warmth of your palms. You can now open your eyes slowly. You have completed the forgiveness meditation. You have forgiven others as well as yourself. Smile and sit in silence. Feel the blessings all around you. This is such a lovely world. So many magical happenings are waiting to catch your attention. Allow them to enthral you. Be kind to yourself. Allow the world around you to shower its kindness on you and show you the love and care you deserve."

MM was silent now. I was sitting quietly with my eyes closed. I was feeling a sense of relief. Finally, she had gone from my life forever. I was like a free bird, ready to soar high in the sky again. I did not have any ill will about her or anyone else who had hurt me. I had blessed her and let her go.

I was feeling blessed and was ready to go back to my world of duties.

♋

Next day, I had my last session with MM.

I asked the question which was hovering in my mind since the last few days.

"I know I have to choose a career or field of passion and devote my time and energy in the same field to channelize my energy so as to get rid of the current frame of mind. I need to start doing something meaningful and something which brings me money. But, what should it be? I am not sure whether I should join the corporate world and build my life there or do something which will not give me the paycheck, at least initially, but will give me happiness, satisfaction and a sense of purpose."

MM asked me, "How old are you?"

"Twenty-six," I said with bit of surprise in my voice.

"I will tell you. But one more question if you do not mind," he was smiling again.

"How long do you want to live? I mean how many years do you want to live on this earth?" MM was smiling again. He had peace prevailing on his face. Gradually, his expressions became serious and his gaze more intense. Now, he looked a little unnerving.

"Eighty-five years, I think…" I blurted out as if to avoid facing his intense gaze.

"Okay. Now can we both close our eyes? Slowly and calmly. Close your eyes and take a deep breath. We will do a small visualisation exercise now. You have to imagine that you are eighty-five years old. You have turned old and are lying on the deathbed. It could be a bed in the hospital. Think of your last day of life. You know that your last time has come and you are going to leave this world within the next twenty-four hours. This is your last chance to think about your life and see all that your eyes can see. Unless you believe in reincarnation, today is your last day and then you vanish in the unending limits of the universe. Visualise. Visualise deeply!"

I could hear the words of MM coming to a silent pause. Then, there was a 'when you hear your own breathing' kind of silence. We could hear the slow beating of our heart against the walls of the chest and the friction of inhalations and exhalations against the nostrils. I could actually feel the entire path of each breath which I was taking, probably for the first time in my life. I could actually feel how the air entered my nostrils and went deep into my lungs. Then the air came out of the lungs and got dissipated into my surrounding in front of my face.

"Now that you can visualise yourself on your last day in the world, imagine that a young man of twenty-six years enters your hospital room. He comes to you and asks for your advice on how he should lead his life. What would you say to him? Can you please take a deep breath and write it on a piece of paper? You can open your eyes," said MM.

I took a piece of paper and started writing my thoughts.

After five minutes, MM asked me to read what I had written.

*First, follow your heart and do what you feel like doing. It's your life. Do not live it as per others' instructions and directions. Once again, this is your life and you have the freedom to live it your way. This is important to become great.*

*Second, love your family, well-wishers and friends and give them your quality time. By quality time, I mean giving them your full attention, care and love.*

*Third, leave a legacy for others to be inspired from your life. Leave this world a little better than it was before you came to life.*

"Okay, now it's time to make your life simple. You are the same twenty-six-year-old young man. You just do the same which you have read out from that page." MM had a calm smile on his face. I was looking at the same paper, on which I had written the keywords, in a new light now.

Now I had to live the way I had written on the paper.

I closed my eyes and tried focussing on the changes I was supposed to make in my life.

I was thinking of first calling my family and talking to them. I had decided to ask for forgiveness from my father who was suffering along with me to see his only son living a life of pain and agony. My days and nights had been invested in choosing the right kind of bouquets and gifts for the girl who had finally ditched me. And my loving family was completely ignored all along.

What a stupid person I truly had been! I opened my eyes with tears in it.

"You are crying...?" MM said with empathy and love in his voice, "Let your tears come out. These tears are special as they are for your own family. All these months, you have been shedding tears in the memory of someone else. You never thought of the pain your family has gone through. You forgot about the teachers who taught you in your childhood days and who also saw dreams for your success. You thought that your life is your life alone. This is not true. Your life and your decisions are also having a deep impact on many others. Let these tears flow. I will leave this hall for some time. You can spend some time alone while thinking about the direction in which you would like to steer your life ahead," MM gave a smile which was filled with affection before getting up and moving out of the hall.

I took my handkerchief and dried my cheeks, only to see more tears welling up. I got up and went to a wash basin to clean my face. Then I came back and sat at the same place again. I was feeling calmer. I closed my eyes. I sat in silence for a long time. I did not say anything and just allowed whatever thoughts came to my mind. Then I visualised the face of my father and grandparents one by one. I imagined their faces smiling at me.

*I asked for forgiveness from my mother who was no more in this world now.*

*I asked for forgiveness from my father.*

*I visualised the faces of my grandfather and grandmother and touched their feet in my imagination.*

I heard the sound of footsteps. MM had come back.

"Thank you sir, I think there is a change within me as I leave you today. I would like to keep your company forever. I bow my head in front of you in gratitude," I said to the coach while leaning before him.

I had received a WhatsApp message from Jayesh, giving the details of my next destination. I had to take a cab to Jaipur and catch a flight from there for Pune.

I was sad to leave MM's company. I was also happy to be leaving for Pune, the city I loved and lived in.

*But where in Pune did Jayesh want me to see him after completing the game of life?*

Pune, here I come in my 2.0 version.

# 9

## Meeting Renee

When I landed at Pune airport, something about me had changed permanently. I was no more the same person. I had realised that the door to happiness, success and enlightenment open from within us. If we feel transformed from within, the world outside looks more splendid. However, like the ignorant musk deer, we keep looking for the mantras of greatness outside us. We blame others, just like I blamed the person who had deserted me. Instead of blessing her for those lovely moments which she had given me, I was acerbic towards her and in the process I had smeared my own life through negative thoughts.

Next day, I got another message from Jayesh. He wanted to check whether I was ready to reach the next destination. Next day was yet another exciting day for me when I had to meet a woman who was an expert in dealing with human relationships.

So finally I was in front of the relationship counsellor's office. I was standing on the road in front of the office of 'Ambrosian Centre of Happiness'. ACH, as it was known in short, was located on Shivneri Road in Pune. The road was full of vehicles. I could see many two wheelers with couples enjoying a joyride. Instead of crossing the road, I took a step back. Though I had come to this road for the first time, something looked familiar.

I saw a huge replica of a heart made in red bricks beside the road. It had an arrow passing through it. It read, "Love heals." Interestingly, the sculptor had first written, "Love hurts." Then, the sculptor struck off 'hurts' and wrote 'heals'. So, finally it read, "Love Heals".

I remember, two years ago, the girl who had deserted me now, had shown me a picture of her with a few other friends. I liked the background of an arrow piercing the heart. When asked where it was taken, she had told me it was on Shivneri Road where she had gone for some shopping with her friends.

I had completely forgotten my conversation with her long ago. But today, I was standing at the same place. In a flash of a second, old memories came rushing back.

Some of her messages from last couple of years started floating in front of me as I stared at the heart pierced by the arrow.

*Hey, a sweet day ahead. So when are we meeting in the evening?*

*I could not sleep till late in the night. Was thinking about you and your sweet messages whole night.*

*You are amazing. Your messages keep me awake.*

*I have to go to college but I don't feel like. I feel like sleeping in the bed and thinking about you the whole day.*

*The rose bouquet which you gave me has been staring at me and reminding me of the beautiful dinner we had last weekend.*

*Yesterday, I met Rupali. You know Rupali? She is my best friend. I don't know whether I told you about her. She was surprised to see a glow on my face. She said, I am looking more beautiful nowadays. She asked me with a smile, is it love? You know what I said? I said, it indeed is love...no dove-wove...ha ha ha!*

*You are the anchor in my life. I do not know how I could have lived without you. I just love you so much. I thank god for having sent you in my life.*

*You know, I was reading a book. It's a love story. I think the boy in the love story is like you. I could imagine your face all the time while reading the book... You surround my world now.*

*I loved the walk that we had in the garden a week ago in the evening. It was getting dark. There were just few people but holding your hands and walking with you was so reassuring. I was feeling so loved, cared for and secured. I will never forget the touch of your palms on mine. It was just so romantic.*

My thoughts were broken by the honking of a bus. It brought me back from the fairyland where the mortal remains of my sweet old past were kept. I stepped back from the road to the footpath. I touched the core of my eyes. It was welling up with tears. I took a handkerchief from my pocket and dried up my eyes. More tears came out. I dried up some more and took some deep breaths in a bid to look normal again. My eyes were hurting and looked red when I saw my face in my selfie camera.

It made me feel even worse. My selfie camera, which was an instrument to take romantic pictures with my girl, had now become a mirror to check my tears!

Times do change.

"What... you don't carry a handkerchief?" I remember how she had laughed at me when she caught me using my shirt to clean my spectacles. That was many months ago and after that day, I made it a habit to carry a handkerchief with me. She often used to tease me, telling me that I needed to be well-groomed.

Did she know that someday later I will need the handkerchief so badly?

Earlier, I used this piece of cloth to clean my spectacles. Now, I use it to clean up traces of my tears.

Memories of the past had once again started pulling me into the same dark zone I wanted to forget and ignore.

Inspiring words of Mr Mehta, the monk, the Naturopathy doctor and the Miracle Man had started vanishing in oblivion.

That is how we get sucked in the whirlpool of negativity with just one wrong thought. True, life can change in a moment, with just one thought.

I could have been lost in my thoughts had I not realised that it was time for me to go to the counsellor's office.

♋

As I entered the office, I could not stop noticing the wall displays with quotations of some great personalities. All the quotations were related to heartbreak and relationships. These were framed along with a picture of the great personality. I first went to the receptionist and told her about my appointment. She asked me to sit for sometime in the lounge until my turn came. I came back and took one of the chairs along the wall.

*Just believe that the heartbreak was a gift in itself. Cry if you have to, but it won't be forever! You will find love again, and it will be even more beautiful! In the meantime enjoy all that you are!"- Rihanna.*

Heartbreak, like any other phase in life, also passes soon. People say, "Time is the biggest healer". This is not true completely. If time were the greatest healer, many people who commit suicide after suffering from heartbreak, would still have been alive. Time alone cannot, and will not, cure all pains. In many cases, people carry a psychological 'dent' throughout their life. If time had been a healer, these circumstances would not have been real.

I had been thinking about the quote for a long time. The phase will pass, but if one wants to avoid any short-term or long-term implications, it is better to have an intervention, surround yourself with some good friends and meet a counsellor.

I saw another frame. It was even more empowering and motivating. It was a quotation by Oprah Winfrey.

*I actually shed tears for the woman I used to be. How sad was I in my 'please' and 'you don't understand, just give me another chance' and all that stuff. What I now know is that was my biggest teacher. He was here to show me to myself so I could learn to love myself more. This was the guy who said to me, 'The problem with you is you think you are special.' And I said, 'No I'm not. No, I'm not really special.' Look at me now.*

This is a powerful statement. We all change as a person with time, and later on, when we look back, we feel bad at the person we used to be. The version 2.0 repents at the version 1.0 of us. However, if we do not get transformed and remain the same version 1.0, we will not even know the person that we could have become and hence there is no question of repentance or surprise. We all must evolve as a person and keep changing ourselves. We must learn from the past mistakes, make new habits, set new goals, correct old weaknesses and build new qualities. That is the true definition of self-transformation.

Oprah's message also has another powerful point. Nobody has ever achieved any great success while being in a state of desperation. The world will turn its face away from you if you show desperation. Oprah was deeply in love with a man who saw her desperation to keep him in her life. He moved on after breaking her heart. But in the process, she understood the meaning of self-love. She knew why it was so important for her to love herself rather than spending all her love on others.

The last part of her message is the most impactful. Often, in our life, we come across people who do not believe in others. These people show off their own confidence, but will never be at ease with the other person's talents. These people hate you for your greatness. They will envy you and will try to demean or denigrate your own personality. At times, they will try to shatter your self-confidence so that their own confidence gets a boost.

It is surprising how the man in Oprah's life alleged her about thinking too much of herself. Ultimately, Oprah became a celebrity. This proves the power of self-confidence and not losing trust in one's own abilities. A heartbreak actually proved to be a blessing in Oprah's life and this was possible because Oprah had the mindset of a winner. She worked on her personal development and never took the demeaning feedback from her ex partner to heart.

I saw another frame even as I saw my turn coming closer with people ahead of me going to meet the counsellor, coming out of her cabin and leaving the hall.

One quote on the right side of the wall read, *"Take your broken heart, make it into art."* Carrie Fisher had said this to Meryl Streep.

When you lose someone, the torrents of energy you feel within can be transformed into a powerful piece of art, which would never have happened had the breakup not occurred. The world is full of many people who transformed their mindset and life to such a level after suffering in their relationships that they became some of the most inspiring personalities. Abraham Lincoln and Oprah Winfrey are just two of many such names.

"Mr Rohan, you can meet ma'am now." I heard the receptionist's voice.

I stood up and walked over to the closed door of the counsellor's office.

"Welcome, Mr Rohan. How can I help you?" the lady on the other side of the table said with a pleasant and calm smile.

"Thank you for your time and attention. I have read a lot about your expertise on advising people on how to fix their life. I have had a broken piece in my life which I want to fix...."

"You can call me Renee. My name is Renee Grewal," she said with a smile. I think a warm and friendly smile is one of the ways for a counsellor to put her clients at ease.

"Sure Renee. It's a pleasure to meet you. I have had a breakup a few months ago. I have been through a journey of finding the pieces of my life. I am collecting my life back. I have gone to a few places and met some of the most accomplished people. I have travelled across the country, but then I thought of meeting an expert who deals specifically with the area of how to mend one's heart when it is broken. I need some advice and guidance from you on this," I said.

"Great, can you tell me something about the story of your life? Something about your background and then about the problem which you are facing now?" Renee asked.

I briefed Renee about me and told her about how I felt when I lost the love of my life. I took a few minutes while narrating my life story and she paid full attention.

"Thanks, Mr Rohan," she said.

"You can also call me by my first name…simply Rohan." I smiled. She laughed.

"Okay Rohan. The first thing, be kind to yourself. It is natural to feel confused at this stage of life. It is not easy to come out of a breakup. In fact, research indicates that recovery from a breakup is similar to getting out of an addiction. We get addicted to a person in life. When the person leaves us, we face similar symptoms, which a person in a de-addiction centre goes through. It is known as 'Addiction Withdrawal Symptoms' or AWS and it is not an easy phase of life.

"Just as a drug addict craves for a dose of drug while withdrawing from the addiction, a person coming out of a breakup yearns for the lovely old days when they had experienced bliss. These sweet memories of life get embedded in our mind and we tend to miss them for a long time. Hence, the first thing I would advise is to take it easy and accept that it's okay to feel the pain. Just be kind to yourself and give yourself the time to heal. Having said that, always remember that the person you were in love with, was not an ideal person, though you always thought so. The person who decided to move away from your life had her own weaknesses and darker side.

"I always suggest to my clients to make a list of the shortcomings of the other person. They first get surprised, but once they start writing, they can fill many pages while listing the problem areas of the other person. Now, your mind has to accept that neither the person with whom you had a relationship was ideal, nor your relationship with the person was a spotless one. This is true with all relationships in the world. This is the way life is. Hence, take a chart and write down about the dark side of the person. Write down her shortcomings. Keep this paper at a place where you can see it every time you start feeling the pain.

"We all make mistakes in life. Nobody has attained anything great without making mistakes. Failures are the stepping-stones to success. The breakup is also like a failure in your relationship and this also is meant to make you stronger and wiser in life. I am sure you must have realised that after falling out of the relationship, now you can pay more attention to your life, work and studies. It will make you sad initially, but the pain is the way to gaining ultimate peace." She took a pause to have a glass of water. I was listening to her with unwavering attention. Then, she continued.

"Let me tell you the story of Mira. She was diagnosed with cancer in her left breast when she was just twenty years old. She went through intense chemotherapy for months, only to come back to normal health at a fast pace. She was happy in life once again after having won this battle when she felt a lump in her right breast. Again, she had to go through the same treatment for the next few months. She braved this phase in life and came out a winner. After some time she fell in love with a person and went for a phase of intense dating. After a year or so, when she was expecting the guy to propose to her, the person decided to breakup with her. To her shock and horror, the person left her life at a time when she thought her life was finally going to turn into a fairy tale, just the way she had seen in some of the romantic movies. You won't believe, she struggled for many months and still could not cope with this. A brave girl who did not accept defeat against cancer, was about to lose the battle of life after a breakup."

As she spoke, I was listening to her in amazement. I could not believe her words.

"Rohan, I always say that going through a breakup is not a journey, it's a fight and you have to put up this fight with all your might. The good news here is, you can surely win this battle. I made the same suggestion of keeping the list of weaknesses of her ex-boy friend in her phone and see it occasionally. And then, she recovered, that too very fast. She realised that it was not an ideal relationship. She also started practising meditation and some of the morning rituals before she forgot this episode of life and moved on with her studies and career. She also found love again soon. She set new goals in her life to keep her busy and focussed. She is happily married now," Renee looked at me after taking a pause.

"Great, can you tell me more about the meditation and spiritual practices which can help heal a broken heart?" I asked.

"Yes, why not! You can simply sit and focus on breathing. You can sit and listen to whatever sound you hear. You can sit in silence and focus on your body organs and thank them for making your life healthy. You can close your eyes and just focus on how pure oxygen is entering your nostril and impure carbon dioxide is leaving your body. There are many ways to do meditation. I am sure you must have learnt a few types from your mentors and gurus whom you met in the last few weeks. You can choose any meditation type that you like. These practices have a deep impact on one's thought process and help one heal faster. I can send you a few links, which are on my official website. You will get an email with these links. Please go through all of these. You will realise how powerful these links could be," Renee said with a beaming smile.

I could see how proud she was about her pursuit of helping so many people like me.

She further said, "Let me share another story with you. This story is that of a woman who had planned a second honeymoon with her husband after twenty years of marriage. But on the day of breaking the news to her husband, she got the shock of her life when her husband told her about his intention to seek divorce. The woman was left devastated.

She was in the state of disillusionment and depression for two days before thinking of moving ahead with the second honeymoon trip. The only difference was, she was alone on her honeymoon trip. It was a trip to Zambia. First, she went to the hotel in the capital city of Lusaka where she stayed in a five-star hotel for a day. On the second day, she was flown into one of the forests of Zambia to live in a tent in an elephant conservation zone. A group of people had a common purpose of protecting baby elephants in case poachers killed the parents. Once the baby elephant was raised for a few months to be able to stay safe on its own, it was left in the forest.

"When the woman reached the forest, she saw a baby elephant, which was on the verge of dying as its mother was killed by the poachers and without care and food, the baby would not have stayed safe on its own. The woman realised that god had sent her to this place with some intention as she was actually a veterinary doctor who had left her practice many years ago to look after her husband and raise their child. She volunteered to attend to the baby elephant in a critical stage and after couple of days, the little animal was back on its feet in a state of good health.

"This gave a purpose to the woman. She felt delighted to be the reason behind the protection of the baby elephant and this helped in alleviating the pain of separation that she was going through. A renewed sense of purpose together with the newfound joy of saving little animals in the forest, gave her a new boost of motivation to resurrect her life, and soon, she found love in another good human being. Is it not an interesting story on how to come out of a breakup?" Renee said, smiling her signature sweet smile.

I was intrigued by the story. I nodded in affirmation. It was clear that the story was convincing and had a few interesting changes which I also could have made in my life.

"This is the story of the movie, *Holiday in the Wild*. You must watch this and some other movies I will share the names of," Renee added.

I replied. "This is interesting, ma'am. I also need to find a purpose in my life. After all, any moment of adversity does have a seed of transformation in it. Heartbreak is one of the most intense forms of adversity and I am sure this can be used to change ourselves completely. In fact, I have been to a few places across the country and have learnt quite a few things in my journey. Maybe the person who sent me to you has designed the sequence of places in a well-thought out manner. I can now get the final touch of positivity and advice, which will help me resurrect my life completely. And now I can also inspire your clients if you suggest.

"It is a great privilege for me to share happiness around the world. If you see value in what I am doing, may be you can allow me to work for you. Probably, I will get the same happiness, which the lady veterinary doctor got while bringing a baby elephant to life."

"Great Rohan. Additionally, you must write four to five goals of your life. You can write the goals on a time horizon of three months, six months, one year, three years, five years and ten years. For example, write multiple goals and keep them written and painted on a chart paper in front of your eyes. Maybe, you can paste the goal sheet on a wall in your room where you can see these every day. A life without goals is like undertaking a road trip without knowing which place to go. It's meaningless, in fact. Why don't you do this? Please prepare a presentation of your journey of self-transformation and also include your goals. Then we can meet sometime next week. Let's discuss the way forward then?" she said.

"Thanks Renee. Yes, let's meet soon," I chuckled and got up to shake hands.

In the evening I got another message from Jayesh.

> *Hope you liked meeting Renee. She is my friend and she did tell me that you are recovering impressively. She wants to share your story of transformation with others. Great going! Now, a surprise! Though I had told you about five places initially and you have visited all of these by now. Well, it's yet not completed. I believe in delivering more than I promise. Hence, though I told you to visit five places, here is a surprise.*
>
> *You have to visit one more place before we meet. This is the sixth and last place that you would be visiting. And then the game of life ends. We will meet over a coffee in Pune. But before we meet, here are*

*your tickets to visit Bengaluru. I am sure you will enjoy your trip to the musical place. Rest, we will discuss when we meet. Do let me know if you face any issue. Though there should be none. You know by now, I am an expert travel planner. :-)*

*Love,*
*Jayesh*

I had a smile while reading the message from Jayesh. Delivering more than you promise! Interesting!

♋

I thought of sleeping early. But even after I switched off the lights, memories of her eyes getting overwhelmed with emotions as I narrated my poem dipped in my innocent love for her came alive. The same memories flashed after I closed my eyes.

Love is an addiction. The game of life to me was actually like being in a de-addiction centre. I was showing withdrawal symptoms. Her memories in the flashback often seared through my calm heart otherwise.

I did not know when I slept that evening, but it took some time before I went to sleep.

Once again, I felt overwhelmed by the memories of love, which was no more in my life.

# 10

## The Piano Museum

I woke up next day with a call from Jayesh. It was late in the morning. My head was still reeling from the sleepless night I had last evening. I disconnected his call and messaged him that I will call him back.

After washing my face, I sat for meditation for some time and did some breathing exercises. I started feeling lighter. I practised some incantation about happiness and energy and to my surprise, I actually started feeling better in an instant.

Then I called Jayesh.

"Hi Rohan. How are you? Hope all is going great. Today, I have got the sixth and last challenge for you. It's a bonus challenge. I am so happy that you have completed all the challenges which I gave you before. You are a winner, man! Just imagine, you are not even twenty-six years of age and you have already visited some great places in different states. Each place must have been unique and more exotic than the other! Now coming to the last challenge of the game for you. By the way, hope you are doing well," Jayesh paused for a moment. He was always in a state of high energy.

"I am good Jayesh. With some practice, I know I will be feeling great and all the credit goes to you," I said with a light smile on my face.

"Sure Rohan. Now, coming to the challenge which I spoke about; it is a musical challenge. You would be visiting a truly incredible museum now. This is in Bengaluru. You will get the tickets for it soon. Have a great tour, my dear friend. After you are back from the place, we will meet over coffee. Now, I need to stop here. Bon voyage," he disconnected the phone after a pleasant goodbye.

I got the WhatsApp message from Jayesh afterwards. It had flight tickets to Bengaluru. The envelope also had an all-inclusive ticket of 'Interactive Music Museum' in J P Nagar.

I was surprised, as I never knew there could be a museum dedicated entirely to music in the country. Soon, I was all geared up to spend a day in the music museum.

In my childhood days, I had composed some music so that I could sing my self-composed songs in the annual school cultural event. I was really appreciated in those days as I was the only student in the school who never sang a song from a movie. I had my original creation of music. I used to write songs and poems and sang them to my own tunes.

But that was many decades ago. As I grew up, layers of dust were deposited on my love for writing and singing. Even though it was my childhood passion, I had forgotten to rekindle it.

♋

As I boarded the flight to Bengaluru, I started thinking of how and why I lost my passion for music.

*But was it my true passion? How to discover one's passion? How to be sure of what my true passion was?*

Hey, that's a good sign. For the first time ever since I fell in and out of love, I had been thinking about what I truly loved doing. What my true passions were!

Looks like, finally I was coming out of the edge of the mist into open air. I want to dedicate my talents and energy to the field of greatness and success. I want to dedicate my strengths to my passion to make it bigger. But what could that field be?

♋

I reached Bengaluru and checked into a hotel. It was late in the afternoon. Next day, I was to go to the musical museum. I thought of taking rest in the hotel and ordered some room service. While eating, I switched on the TV and saw the interview of one of the greatest sports coaches of all times, Patrick Mouratoglou.

"I could never speak a word during my childhood days in my school. The mere sight of people in school used to scare me. I used to experience a fear of saying something and I did not know what that sentence would be. I always experienced panic attacks while looking at people. This was a severe weakness for me. I went to a child psychologist for one year to get my fear of public speaking treated. But it took me one year to say a word.

"Yes, one full year to say one word. That is how serious the matter was. But this universe has many secrets within it. Your weaknesses can turn into your biggest strengths and that is what I saw happening with me. My fear of beginning a conversation with my classmates made me sit silently in the classroom, but it did something very interesting to me as a child. I always used to watch others in conversation. I kept staring at the faces of people and see their expressions and emotions. I was terrible at striking a conversation, but I became adept at reading people.

"Later, my ability became the most important quality as a coach. I enjoyed observing people, seeing their movements, reading their facial expression and connecting these to their actions and the way they play tennis. My fear became my greatest strength. Today I coach the greatest tennis players and this ability to observe and learn about the strength and weaknesses of people helps me remain at the top of my profession," said Patrick Mouratoglou.

Patrick has been coaching Serena Williams since 2012.

It is interesting to note that Patrick initially wanted to become a tennis player. He had the passion for tennis but somehow could not become a great player. Then he turned his focus towards becoming the coach, which worked out perfectly for him.

Often, we do not know our true strengths. Finding your passion and talent is a matter of trial and error. You have to take a lot of actions and gradually you come closer to your passion and talent.

This got my thoughts running. Had I done enough self-exploration to discover my talents and qualities? There was no rule book to find one's talents. You just need to listen to your inner voice and do some research.

Why don't I write the things which are close to my heart? Maybe, that will take me closer to my answer. I picked up a pen and paper and began noting down various possibilities.

*I can become a relationship counsellor. For this, I will need to get a professional qualification.*

*I can become a life coach for people who are suffering from difficult experiences in life and are finding it difficult to come out of the trauma.*

*I can become an author who can write books to inspire youngsters and help them come out of their relationship related traumas. I love writing my thoughts, though I have never written anything more than a few pages at a time.*

*I can join a professional institution and get a professional degree or qualification to join an organisation and do more.*

*I can learn the art and science of entrepreneurship and begin my own business.*

*I can become a motivational speaker to inspire people to use their heartbreaks as the seed of their greatness and success. I can develop a niche for myself in this field as hardly there are any motivational speakers who speak to inspire youngsters who have gone through a breakup. This could create a niche area for me. I can also use my passion and talent for music and poetry to inspire people.*

*I can become someone who is both a writer and a musician.*

♋

My visit to the museum proved to be a soulful and spiritual experience for me. Ages had passed since I came so close to doing something I always loved.

The world has two types of forces – visible and invisible. When someone forbids access to something we love, it's a visible force. Our emotions become the invisible force, which prevent us from doing many things we should have done or we originally wanted to do. My falling in love with the girl became one such invisible force, which kept me away from numerous other things which were important. I was immersed in a world of my own with my girlfriend and focussed only on all the things which made *her* happy.

While standing in front of a huge piano in one of the largest halls in Bengaluru, I realized how I had lost my identity. Love had indeed made me blind.

The museum had three distinct areas. In the first area, people got a basic idea as how music is created. This area did not have any musical instrument but was made up of different materials like metal, wood and stone. There was a hollow stone, inside which you could insert your head and chant *om*. As I did so, I could feel the vibrations and resonance all through my body. I felt as if the sound of *om* was cleansing my heart, mind and body.

I felt as if I was becoming a new person who was about to find his way back. After spending many months in the false pursuit of the mirage of love, I was now getting ready to live a life which god had wanted me to live and love.

There was another zone in the museum where you could strike metal panels of different sizes and create different types of music. You could see how musical this entire universe and nature is. There is music in the swaying of breeze, babbling sound of water and brushing of tree leaves with each other.

*Finally, I was ready to pick the lost music in my life. Music, which I loved. Music, which I always yearned for. Music, which I worshipped.*

As I spent some more time in the museum, I understood why Jayesh had planned my trip there. It was a surreal feeling to stand in the hall, which had nothing but pianos all around me. I was like Alice in wonderland for the whole day. I was joyous and excited like a ten-year-old child who had got a bagful of his favourite chocolates. I could feel connected with my true childhood passion of music. I sat in front of pianos and played the music for a long time.

After coming back to the hotel, I wrote in detail about my childhood passions, which always made me happy. Today, I got a meaningful insight.

*Everyone talked of falling in love as one of the blessings of life, but no one said that falling out of love could also be a bigger blessing! Falling out of love could be similar to drinking a bowl of boiled herbs and spices known as 'kadha'. It tastes bitter, but is good for your health. Today, I realized that falling out of love could also be good for health, wealth and happiness. Well not immediately, but surely after some time.*

# 11

## *Jayesh's Calling*

"So dude, now it's time for us to have a cup of coffee. You suggest a place and we will meet there over this weekend. Take some rest now. I am sure you must have been tired of travelling across the country. You are a winner. But winners also need to take a break. I am sure your travel to Bengaluru must have been great. But we will talk about this and more when we meet in Kasturgaon. I am sure you are feeling a change within you. Let's meet in Starbucks Café this Sunday. Do not forget."

Jayesh's call followed me as soon as I landed at the Pune airport. He wanted to know and discuss everything.

The next two days went documenting all that I had seen, felt and experienced over the last few weeks in my journal. I had gone through a range of new experiences and wanted to write it all.

Like a film's reel, all the memories were moving in front of my eyes. It became so easy for me to write my thoughts and perspectives. To be candid, I do not know what propelled me to write. I think when you go through a flood of emotions of various kinds, it becomes easy for you to write.

My story began on the day when I had collapsed on the floor of the room after seeing her with someone else. It was the day when my knees were shivering and could not support me. I was physically healthy, but mentally I was so devastated to see her being with someone else that all the blood in my veins turned into streams of pain. The reel moved to the moment my phone rang and subsequently moved to all the major destinations of the game of life that I participated in.

Writing one's ideas and memories could be such a creative process!

♋

I was meeting Jayesh after many years. We met over coffee at Starbucks where I was to meet Analia, few years later. I hugged Jayesh as I saw him outside the café and thanked him for doing all that he had done for me.

"So this was supposed to be your last game, Rohan. I had told you that you are free to choose your path ahead in life after going through this game. You appear to be a new man now. I hope you have also started believing in the philosophy of reincarnation. So over to you now as I enjoy my coffee," Jayesh smiled and took the mug of coffee in his hands.

"I don't know when and how it started changing. I mean, the way I was looking at my life changed. You were right; your company makes all the difference. As I started visiting new places and meeting new people, who were some of the wisest people around, I started seeing a change within me. I started seeing endless possibilities in my future. I started witnessing a new world opening around me. I realised that we create our own world based on our mindset. If we are inspired by a great purpose, we create a world of inspiration around us. If we are dispirited, we create a world of negativity around us. That was quite a revelation for me."

"What were you thinking when you accepted to play the last game?" Jayesh stopped sipping his coffee for a moment.

"I was on the verge of taking a plunge into darkness just before you called me. I was almost on the cliff, looking down the valley of death. When you challenged me to play the last game, initially I was totally against it. I think, your ability to inspire others worked wonders and after talking to you for a while, I thought of giving it a chance. I was not going to lose anything. You motivated me to take a step behind and look at life once again. I had the freedom to come back to the same cliff and jump, never to come back again, right into its eyes. But how did you convince me?" I paused and reached out to take a sip.

"Rohan, I did not tell you in detail, but I am a motivational speaker and life transformation coach. I have coached many people to their success and happiness. Many of my mentees were like you and I knew I had to somehow change the pattern of your thinking. I was so persistent in cajoling you to accept the challenge of the last game because I knew otherwise you would have lost the battle of life while meandering alone in the dark and endless tunnel. I knew you had turned suicidal and that evening could have been your last evening had someone not spoken with you. You had lost your purpose in life. I had to create some excitement for you. I had to give you a nudge. I had to give you one reason to live. I had to make you chase some goals in life with deadlines in the near future. That would have made you look forward to life. At that moment, I had to make you look up and accept the challenge thrown by me," Jayesh said.

"And you did it so intelligently and beautifully," I said.

"I did so because I knew the outcome of this game. I can share with you another secret now. I have made many people go through this game of life. I did it for many of my mentees who had lost meaning in their life. I have been making them go through the same route on which I had travelled for two full years when I decided to explore the secrets of this world. The people you have met are my gurus and mentors. I have spent at least one month while being in the company of each of them. I discovered the real me and the secrets of this world while being in their company. I had taken a sabbatical for one year after going through a devastating experience myself.

"Based on what I have experienced, I knew that if I could become a life coach while learning from them, you can surely change your life after meeting them. Every mentor spent some good personal time with you, despite being surrounded by a large number of wellness seekers because I had requested them all to do so, seeing the criticality of the situation. You needed focussed attention. In fact, I have a large team working with me. The team organises these trips for my mentees so that they don't face any trouble. That is why you had such a smooth journey," Jayesh had finished his coffee.

"But how did it all start? I mean, how did you think of calling me?" This is one question that I always wanted to ask. By now, I was in awe of what Jayesh was doing.

He smiled as if he was to take the lid off a long-kept secret.

"I had called your father to return the loan. I am earning well from my coaching business and now it was time to return money to your father. I called your father. Uncle sounded sad when I spoke with him. Being in this field, I can understand a lot from the intonation of people. I probed a bit and came to know about you being critically depressed. He was afraid of losing you forever as you had stopped responding to his calls. He was not sure if you would explain your situation to me. He was also not sure if you would take my call. Hence, an idea occurred to him. It was probably his last chance to save his sinking son. He asked me to call you and tell you about the money which I had to return to him. He knew that you would not be interested in money. He asked me to engage you in conversation. The idea was to distract your mind away from negative thoughts and feelings.

"It was long since you had spoken with any of your friends and my call might bring a change in your thinking. This is what uncle was anticipating. I had become a life coach and motivational speaker after undergoing a similar experience in my life. I never told you, but I also was in love with a girl for many years, only to see her dying just before marriage. I was in severe depression before a wise person asked me to take a break and meet some of the people whom you have already met. And my life changed for ever from there. Hence, I knew it would work for you as well."

"This is interesting. The monk in Himalayas, MM the coach in Pushkar and the Naturopathy and Yoga guru in Yogic Village and others like them... you have met all of them," I kept the coffee mug on the table.

"Yes! We wanted to keep the element of surprise in the game. Now you see an interesting truth of this world. This is known as the law of attraction. Thoughts become things. You invite people, thoughts and life situations as per your thinking. You, me, monk, coach, yoga guru, Mr Mehta – we all are connected with a common thread. We all have undergone a deep personal experience and hence can feel for each other. This is known as the law of attraction. Your company influences your life and this is one of the many principles of the game of life." Jayesh smiled.

"I wish we had more people like you who could have guided others like me," I said.

"I have been trying to reach out to as many people as possible. My job is to sow the seed of positivity in the minds of people like you. It is this seed which you need the most at such a critical phase of life. This changes the pattern of your thinking. What I have seen is that such a call is like a nucleus around which further layers of positivity start getting deposited. I am saying so from my experience. That initial nucleus or seed is essential. That is how the pearl of positivity was created in your life. I can feel the shine of this pearl on your face.

"I can feel the shine of this pearl in your heart and mind. Your words, your smile, your confidence, the strength of your purpose – all of this has the shine of a pearl. I am happy that I became that tiny nucleus around which the layers of positivity started getting formed. As a famous poet has rightly said, a journey of a thousand miles begins with a single step. My call to you was that first step.

"Rohan, you always had the power within you. You have been a great receiver of goodness and positivity. I was a transmitter, but unless the receiver was powerful enough, my calls or talks would not have had any impact. You have proven that positivity and power could be temporarily covered by the clouds of doubts and worries, but ultimately, it comes out dispelling the mist and fog. Success belongs to those who take action and you have proven that you are an action taker. Your transformation is due to your conviction to change your life. I am going to use your story to inspire others as well. Cheers Rohan, to a great life ahead," Jayesh said.

"Thanks Jayesh. My gratitude to you," I said.

"So what do you want to do in your life? I am sure you have set your life goals..."

"Yes, can you help me to become a life and success coach? I can work with you to learn the art and science of organising the game of life. I have also thought of setting up piano coaching centres. That has been one of my passions in life. So, setting up call centres around the country to help people save their life and starting a chain of piano teaching centres in major cities to let people enjoy their music without spending much... I have many dreams coming in my mind now. I am full of ideas, some of which I am going to work on. I am highly motivated and excited to attain my massive goals and that is a great feeling. I know many people cannot play piano because of its high cost. I want to make it the purpose of my life to let people follow their passion of music."

"Okay, we will discuss this in details in our next call. I will be recommending some courses and studies which you are going to attend. Always learn something new. The journey of becoming your version 2.0 begins now," Jayesh said before getting up to leave.

# 12

## *The Transformation*

I have visited many places around the country and have met some of the wisest people who surmounted various challenges in their life only to channelise these difficult moments to transform their life. I have gone through various phases of transformation while visiting different parts of the country. While the world is living under a cloud of ignorance and mediocrity, people have the tendency to think small.

The world always looks up to those people who have money, power and influence in society. The world does not exude respect for people who form the lowest strata of the society. People think that anyone who wants to grow in life and achieve greater success needs to take the wrong path of crime or deceit. Some of the blockbuster movies and bestselling books are based on the stories of crime, deceit and fraud. The fact is, anyone from any strata of the society can become a great man. The world is full of inspiring stories of people who created miraculously huge business empires from scratch. If they can do so, then why can't others?

During the phase of post-breakup disenchantment, I completely forgot all my strengths and talents. That is what depression and an uninspiring life does to you. Then I started studying the norms of this society closely and discovered some revealing facts. I realised the power and secrets of transformation. I decided to collaborate with NGOs or social groups who could get me an opportunity to address the problems of lack of motivation among people, especially youngsters. I conducted seminars and webinars for large groups of these people to help them transform their mindset and chase bigger goals

Eventually, I became a motivational coach for the country. My seminars used to be attended by lakhs of people. My community started growing by leaps and bounds. I could see thousands of lives changing. I used to conduct free programmes for people who came from the bottom of the social pyramid. Gradually, I had enough money to visit a few countries every year. It was my passion to visit the world and collect lessons of inspiration, growth and success from different parts of the world. I became a 'hunter-gatherer' of motivational stories and principles to succeed. I met many people, visited many cities and read many books to gather hidden nuggets of wisdom, which could transform anyone's life. I applied all these learnings in my life, wrote down the experiences and inspired others to apply these before making these insights a part of my regular curriculum of training programmes and motivational workshops.

I started coaching people on the 'Wheel of Life' which included growth on each of the eight aspects of life, including health, career, money, social life, passion and hobbies, love, recreation and attitude. From being an average-minded person who had a limited impact, I had become a person who made a wider impact on the society. My influence grew in an almost incredible way. Your financial status is a mere reflection of your impact on the society and the value which you add. My financial status became stronger. But what was more gratifying was the fact that I was able to touch the lives of so many people.

But as I had learnt while sketching the wheel of life, I never missed my focus from my passion and hobbies. I played piano in my free time. My visit to the museum of pianos had a long lasting impact on my life. I still play piano as it connects me to the source of my creation. My life is based on two pillars – transformation of the society and piano. I am a pianist who also inspires people.

*Oh, did I tell you about a letter which took me by complete surprise?*

It had been few years since she stepped out of my life. I got this letter a year ago and this was completely unexpected for me. It was a letter from her.

Also, I did not even realise that I am yet to tell you the name of the girl for whom I used to write poems. I did not want to think of her name again as it made me feel terrible.

But today, I am not afraid of taking her name as she has become the seed of transformation in my life. Had she not walked away, I would never have become my present version. People are correct when they say that life does not give anything to you if you are desperate for it. But as you move on, it follows you if it belongs to you. If you are desperate for a job and are scared that you may not get it, it will never come to you. But when you come out of the fear and become a confident person, the same job chases you.

I learnt it after I got this letter from Riya. Well, now you know her name, finally. I am not afraid of taking her name as it does not sadden me anymore. Surprisingly, the letter did not evoke any emotion within me when I got it. I did not expect it and I did not feel happier or sadder. I just smiled. It was evidence, solid proof that I had moved on in my life.

*Dear Rohan,*

*I am sorry.*

*I moved out of your life without giving any explanation. I just sent a WhatsApp message and left, never to meet you again.*

*Often in life, we take a decision, which we do not justify to others. We think our life is ours and others do not have the authority to interfere in it. But later, we realise how big a stake others also have in our decisions. However, by the time we realise the truth, it is too late.*

*After being away from you for more than five years, I was not sure if I should have written this letter to you. But I had a realisation in my life in recent times and understood that any decision that we take in life also has some life-altering impact on important people. Any personal decision, however small or big it is, has an impact on others as well. These people could be our family members, neighbours, friends, well-wishers and even those who do not wish well for us. It took me some time to understand that we need to keep the emotions of others in mind.*

*When I took the decision to move out of your life, I did not realise that I had a moral duty and responsibility to inform you. You had high stakes in my decision. But I did what most of the people in the world do. People have fun together and share some intimate bonds with each other. However, when they part ways, they do not realise that irrespective of the level of bitterness with which they storm out of someone's life, they cannot deny that they have already invested some good time, energy and emotions into the relationship. It is important to inform, explain and discuss everything, moving on their respective paths. This prepares the other person in the relationship to move on with relatively more self-worth, peace, calmness and good feeling for the other person.*

*I got swayed by the ways of the world and did what I shouldn't have done.*

*I have been following you on social media. In one of your recent videos, you said something, which resonated with me. You spoke about the power of decision-making. You said that every day we make many decisions, which can impact the lives of many people. We should spare some time before going to sleep. We should sit in the state of meditation and make a list of decisions that we made on that day. We should always think of the people who are going to be affected by that decision of ours in some way or the other. We should ask a question to ourselves – did we inform the people about our decision in a proactive manner? If the answer is no, we should immediately make a list of such people and inform them either on the same day or include this task in our daily planner for the next day.*

*A realisation dawned upon me. How could I decide to not talk to you before calling off our relationship? You had such a high emotional stake in the decision and yet I chose not to speak with you before moving on.*

*Hence, I decided to pen down this letter to seek your apology.*

*It took me some time to realise that we were two different people. I know I caused pain to you. But, regardless of everything, you stayed positive and moved on with more energy and vigour on your new path.*

*I am incredibly happy to see how well you are doing in your life. I wish you a happy birthday!*

*Keep progressing in life.*

*With best wishes,*
*Riya Ravin Sharma*

This letter was my birthday gift from Riya.

It reminded me of the last birthday gift which I had received few years ago. That was before we parted ways. We were in love then. I smiled while thinking of those old days.

♋

"Hi... I won't let you open your eyes. Please don't force it open. I want you to make a guess. I have a special birthday gift for you. And you have to tell me what it is. I will give you a clue though. Now I am going to turn your face towards the gift," she said and turned my face in a different direction.

"Now you are standing looking at the gift. It is special, as I have told you. You know your birthday has to be very special for me. Hence, the gift is also extremely special." She was chirping like a bird.

I was enjoying the touch of her soft fingers on my eyes. I could feel the slightly warm feeling of her petal-soft fingers on my eyes. I could also feel the cold touch of her ring which I had gifted her last month. The touch of her soft and warm fingers and hard and cold golden ring on my closed eyes was a feeling I still remember. The time stood still for me. She was saying something, chirping and giggling. I could hear the excitement in her voice. But beyond that, I could hear nothing. I was feeling the fragrance of her fingers.

I was lost in the heavenly feeling of her soft and warm fingers, metallic cold finger ring and intoxicating smell of her body.

"Hey, why don't you say something? I have been telling you about the clue and you are just silent," she said in exasperation.

"Oh sorry, can you tell me again?" I asked smilingly.

"The clue is – it is for you but will benefit me," she chuckled.

It turned out to be an iPad. It took me some time to understand what she meant. I loved writing and she loved hearing the poems written about her. So I was to write these poems on the iPad now.

"You have to recite some new poems to me." She smiled.

♋

Riya is not a part of my life anymore. I had gifted that iPad to the son of a poor attendant who was working in Yog Gram. The joy that I saw on the young boy's face when he received the gift was unparalleled. That is when I realized that I had indeed moved on to a better tomorrow.

It has been a year since I had coffee with Analia. While writing my book as advised by her, I have completed the full circle of life. It makes me nostalgic to think of how remarkable a journey life has been for me.

My book is complete and I have sent it to Analia. She has made some pertinent corrections so that the book can take better shape. It is ready for launch amidst marketing and social media campaigns.

Analia has planned a grand book launch party in the city. She has prepared articles about my book, which she would be printing in leading magazines as a part of its promotional campaign. She has also spoken with many relationship counsellors to recommend my book to their patients and clients. Overall, she has done what I could never imagine in my wildest dreams.

I am often surprised why she has been so kind to me. Has she fallen in love with me? Perhaps, yes. Even though it seems like a crazy idea!

But I still cannot stop smiling while looking into the mirror.

I have been looking at the mirror more often nowadays. After all, I need to look charming as there are so many launch parties planned soon.

"Rohan, you look handsome man!" I say to myself while looking into the mirror.

# 13

## *Life Is Beautiful*

"Hi Analia, it is a pleasure seeing you again. It has been more than a year since we met…" I say, while welcoming Analia.

"The pleasure is all mine. You are a superstar now. Your story has become a lighthouse to show the right path to innumerable readers who have also gone through a heartbreak. You are one of the youngest entrepreneurs in the country who has a biography written on his life. Does it not feel surreal to you?" she says excitedly.

"We will talk properly. But let me order a coffee for you. More of milk or more of coffee?" I ask.

"More of milk…Latte," she says with an even bigger smile.

I place the order for two lattes and return to the corner table on the wooden blocks used as sitting chairs. The café is still the same, with branches and leaves of gulmohar tree hanging from all sides. Kasturgaon Park area has not changed a bit since I came here last.

It is a strange feeling. When I fell in love, I felt like I was on top of the world. I felt like the happiest person in the world. I thought I had attained everything. However, when I had the breakup, I became miserable. I felt as if I was the most miserable person in the world.

But today, when I look back, I am shocked to realise how wrong we all can be. The most painful phase of my life has given me the true feeling of happiness.

*Now I know that true happiness is a feeling, which we experience when we utilise our full potential and talents.*

Only then, we can truly connect with god. Only then, we can experience what it means to be in a constant state of 'flow'. Had I not fallen in the darkest valley of sadness and despair, I would have never realised how bright the feeling of happiness could be.

As I ruminate on these thoughts, I sit once again after bringing the coffee to our table.

I can see that Analia is more interested in my story now. She has kept the coffee mug aside and turned once again to me.

"Today I am an author, philanthropist, life coach, relationship counsellor and a pianist. I strive to spread the magic of goodness and music in everyone's life. My book has become a national bestseller. I have opened a chain of piano teaching centres in all major cities in the country. I have started a twenty-four-hour, nationwide helpline for young boys and girls looking for advice, which could save their life. I don't think I could have become any of these had I not fallen out of love and sunk in the dark and gloomy valley of pain and sufferings."

"You are a bestselling author now, Rohan. If I ask you to tell me one turning point of your life, which event would it be?" she asks me.

"I cannot speak of one such turning point. I think I had two turning points in my life," I say while looking out of the windows where a pair of squirrels is running up and down the trunk of a gulmohar tree laden with vibrant red flowers.

"Nature always inspires me. It has invigorated me even more in the last few years since I got that first call. That call was surely the first important seed for my transformation. We look for god in temples, churches and mosques. The places of worship have a positive energy and hence a visit to these places is always good. But god comes to us in various forms and identities. I think, I was blessed when god made a call to me at the right time. He called me in the disguise of Jayesh." I stop for a while as I feel a lump in my throat. I quickly lift my mug and take two large sips of coffee. This helps me clear my voice before it could get choked with emotions.

I continue, "I do not know what would have happened to me had Jayesh not called me. My interaction with him changed the pattern of my thinking. It is like two airplanes taking off from Mumbai airport and keeping a difference of just one degree in their direction. After an hour, one will reach Chennai and the other will reach somewhere else, say Hyderabad. I had a similar experience in my life. That little change in the direction turned out to be transformative for me. I know, making a small change in the way we do things today, makes a gigantic difference later in life....” I pause momentarily to see my coffee mug being empty.

“Hey, I need another cup of coffee. What about you?” I ask.

“Yes, I think it’s all about two today. Two squirrels, two turning points in life and two mugs of coffee...” Analia laughs.

I order the second coffee for both of us and continue, “The second turning point of my life came when I met you.”

“That is interesting, Rohan. It is the first time you have spoken about me. I am curious,” she says as she keeps the mug aside.

“Yes, you heard it right. Meeting you was the second biggest turning point of my life. While giving you the interview, I realised that I also had an inspiring story. You encouraged me to turn the story of my transformation into a book. Often others’ belief in our abilities is stronger than our own self-belief. Your confidence in my story made me think for the first time that I actually have something meaningful to convey to the world. Thank you Analia!”

I take out the new second edition of the book and write on it:

*With my deepest gratitude to Analia, who made this book and miraculous change in my life possible. I dedicate this book to her, who became an angel for me. I had two gods coming to help and she is one of the two.*

I can see tiny droplets of tears in her eyes as she accepts her copy of the latest edition of the book.

"But I want to ask you one thing, Analia. Why did you do all of this for me?" I ask.

I could see that she was brooding. For the first time, she looked a bit emotional. I could see the vulnerable side of her personality instead of the strong professional whom I had met the first time.

"That is a secret I will tell you some other time." She bursts into laughter all of a sudden. I think, this is less of laughter and more of a tactic to hide the true reason. Soon, she is back to her normal professional self.

"I will tell you sometime later. Congratulations once again. May you attain greater heights," Analia gets up to leave. I come out to see her off before calling for my car.

Kasturgaon looks even more beautiful today.

♋

I am still wondering why Analia had tears in her eyes after listening to my story that day. After a few days, I sent a WhatsApp message, reminding her of the secret she had promised to share with me.

There was no reply from her for many days. Days and weeks passed.

And then, one day, her email came.

*Dear Rohan,*

*I had a lovely time writing the foreword of your book. I cannot emphasise enough on how compelling your story is. I have been in the field of mass media for quite some time, so I am fully aware of how marketing and branding acts as a critical tool to enhance the outreach of a product.*

*A great product deserves to reach out to as many people as possible. The problem with this world is not that bad things and people make too much noise. Rather, it is that good people and things remain under the radar and are not able to create the impact which they should make. Every product has to reach out to its target segment of customers or community in a focussed and streamlined way. It is like when we shoot an arrow, we need to have one particular goal in our mind. No archer or shooter has ever succeeded while aiming at more than one target at a time.*

*When I heard you talking about your book, I knew I had to help you so that your book reaches out to its target segment – youngsters. I reached out to good publishers. I ensured that the book is kept at strategic locations in the bookstore. I also made it a point that some promotional material is kept on display to garner attention of people visiting the bookstores. We promoted the book on various social media platforms. Gradually, the book started gaining immense popularity.*

*You must be wondering why I did so much for promoting the book. This is because the powerful message had already reached at least one target reader – me!*

*I had lost my elder brother a few years ago to the same problem. He fell in love with a girl, but could not bear the pain of being rejected by her. He could not accept the fact that the girl, who turned his world into a paradise, also made his life miserable after dumping him for another boy.*

*We tried our best to redirect the focus of my brother to other possibilities and inspire him to move on and look for other things that life had in store for him. Unfortunately, he could not overcome the grief and fell into depression.*

*Six months after the breakup, he was found dead on the rocks beside a river. He had consumed sleeping pills and died while lying on the same rocks where he had first proposed to the girl many years ago.*

*Hence, when I first saw your interview in a magazine, I was touched by how you had transformed your life after having gone through a sorrowful experience. You had every reason to get disenchanted from worldly engagements, but you decided to use this heartbreak to bounce back stronger. What a comeback you have made in your life!*

*I decided to call you to Starbucks to interview you and wanted to publish your story in the most reputed journal which was read widely in the country. I knew that your life story could act as a source of inspiration for others. The interview was well-received and you started getting messages from your readers.*

*Finally, your book came! It was clear that the interview had acted like a seed, which gradually grew into a sapling and then a full-fledged tree.*

*Since I had gone through a similar tragedy, your story resonated with me instantly. I will strive to ensure that your ideas reach as many people as possible. I am glad our path crossed.*

*Looking forward to see you publishing more bestsellers. Keep up the good work!*

*Will see you soon!*

*Best wishes.*
*Analia*

♋

This was my story. I am glad you enjoyed it. You are most welcome to meet me over a steaming cup of coffee anytime at my favourite place – Kasturgaon Park.

Or else, we can meet at my home. As you enter into my living hall, you will see a beautiful painting on one of the walls which has the silhouetted image of a boy standing in a big hall with many open windows and doors through which shining sunrays are filtering in. Through some of the windows, you can see the glimpse of the gulmohar tree with red flowers.

The boy standing in the hall in the painting has a coffee mug in his hands. One door in the hall is closed. But the boy is looking at the doors and windows which are open. He seems to be enjoying his coffee while relishing the warmth of the sun rays.

There is a quote by Helen Keller which is written at the bottom of the painting. It says,

*When one door of happiness closes, another opens; but often we look so long at the closed door that we do not see the one that has been opened for us.*

At the bottom left corner of the painting, the painter has scribbled her name in beautiful cursive hand writing. It reads – Analia Christopher.

Beside her name, there are two little squirrels playing around the fallen leaves and flowers.

Till I got this gift from her, I did not have any clue that she painted so well. This masterpiece will always be close to my heart.

I always believe in surrounding yourself with people who bring out the best in you. Jayesh is one of those people whose company I always cherish.

After all, he is the one who gave me *that phone call* which changed my life forever.

It gave me my twisted love story.

*Recommended Reading*

# THR GIRL IN THE RED LIPSTICK

**Ajay K Pandey**

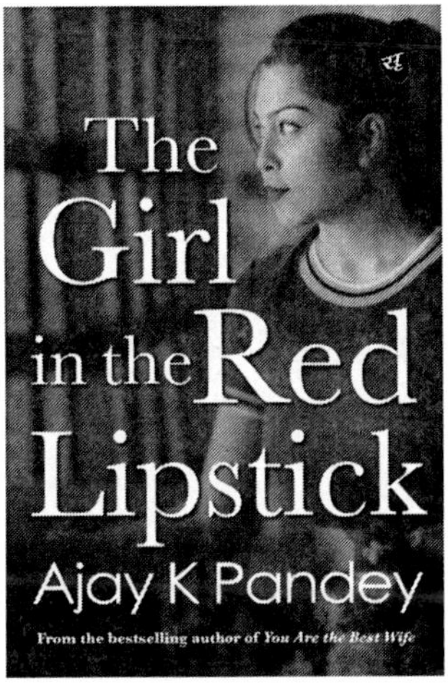


Arun is a bestselling author, and the heartthrob of thousands of readers. While on a book promotion tour, he meets someone with a secret!

Arun sees a story in her, and in digging deeper, is amazed to discover her strength of character. Even though Lalita is a young survivor of human trafficking, she has unmatched determination.

A single encounter with her makes Arun take decisions that he had never even thought of. He is willing to risk everything for her, his own life too.

*The Girl in the Red Lipstick* is a charming story of friendship, life and finding love where we least expect to.

ISBN: 978-9390441310, Pages: 216, MRP:199, Format: Paperback

## THE JOURNEY OF OUR LOVE

**Deesha Sangani**

Anushkaa is a chirpy girl with big dreams and a bigger heart. Abhimanyu is young and dynamic, spearheading his company with gusto.

When they meet, sparks fly! They fall in love with each other's imperfections, walking on the road to love.

ISBN: 978-9390441310, Pages: 216, MRP:199, Format: Paperback

## NOT WITHOUT YOUR LOVE

**Arvind Parashar**

Kabir is a travel journalist, who lands in Afghanistan to find Noosh, the love of his life. Noosh is smart and spirited, and waits for Kabir with bated breath as she works for her country.

Kabir is thrown into the political scene as a spy and finds himself in a conspiracy that will ultimately lead to a war.

ISBN: 978-9390441556, Pages: 224, MRP: 225, Format: Paperback

# MY IMPERFECT LOVE STORY

## Shubhashish Kerketta

Amyra's life turned around completely when the most desirable man in her college, the hot crush of every girl, reached out to her on her twenty-first birthday.

Shashank was older, but flawless.

A poignant story of love, friendship, hatred and revenge, this book will make you smile, break your heart and take you to cloud nine.

ISBN: 978-9390441297, Pages: 200, MRP: 225, Format: Paperback

# THE COCKTAIL OF LOVE

## Dhruv Maloo

Samar is a cartoonist and a hopeless romantic, he thinks mostly from the heart. He falls in love with his best friend Ashna.

Ashna is a budding architect chasing her dreams, living life as it comes. She doesn't want to complicate her precious friendship with Samar.

*The Cocktail of Love* is an electrifying mix of dreams, confusion, commitment and the many shades of love.

ISBN: 978-9390441792, Pages: 200, MRP: 225, Format: Paperback